'You've learnt your lessons well, DePiero...in the beds of however many countless lovers you've entertained. Were they the ones to teach you that intoxicating mix of innocence and artless sensuality designed to ensnare a man?'

Siena looked at Andreas, stunned at his words. He had no idea. He couldn't tell her gauche responses were all too *real*. And she vowed then that he never would know, however she had to do it.

She fought to find some veneer of composure and said, as cynically as she could considering she was shaking inwardly like a leaf, 'What else did you expect? A real *bona fide* virgin heiress? This is the twenty-first century, Xenakis. Surely you know better than most that virgins are as mythical as unicorns?'

Abby Green got hooked on Mills & Boon® romances while still in her teens, when she stumbled across one belonging to her grandmother in the west of Ireland. After many years of reading them voraciously, she sat down one day and gave it a go herself. Happily, after a few failed attempts, Mills & Boon bought her first manuscript.

Abby works freelance in the film and TV industry, but thankfully the four a.m. starts and the stresses of dealing with recalcitrant actors are becoming more and more infrequent, leaving her more time to write!

She loves to hear from readers, and you can contact her through her website at www.abby-green.com. She lives and works in Dublin.

Recent titles by the same author:

EXQUISITE REVENGE
ONE NIGHT WITH THE ENEMY
THE LEGEND OF DE MARCO
THE CALL OF THE DESERT

Did you know these are also available as eBooks?
Visit www.millsandboon.co.uk

FORGIVEN BUT NOT FORGOTTEN?

BY
ABBY GREEN

First published in Great Britain 2013
by Mills & Boon, an imprint of Harlequin (UK) Limited.
Harlequin (UK) Limited, Eton House, 18-24 Paradise Road,
Richmond, Surrey TW9 1SR

© Abby Green 2013

ISBN: 978 0 263 90013 2

Harlequin (UK) policy is to use papers that are natural, renewable and recyclable products and made from wood grown in sustainable forests. The logging and manufacturing process conform to the legal environmental regulations of the country of origin.

Printed and bound in Spain
by Blackprint CPI, Barcelona

FORGIVEN BUT NOT FORGOTTEN?

This is especially for Crispin Green, Polly Green,
Barney Green and Katie Green.
I'm so proud to be your half-sister
and one of the 'Greens in Cornwall'.

PROLOGUE

SIENA DEPIERO HELD her older sister's hand tightly as they left their *palazzo*. Even though she was twelve and Serena was fourteen they still instinctively sought each other for support. Their father was in an even more mercurial mood than usual today. Their car was waiting by the kerb, a uniformed driver standing by the open door. Siena knew that her father's bodyguards were nearby.

Just feet away from the car a tall young man with dark hair seemed to spring from nowhere, stopping their father in his tracks. He was gesticulating and calling their father *Papà*. Siena and Serena had come to a halt too, with burly guards standing between them and this confrontation.

Siena looked around the bodyguards. She could instantly see the resemblance of this young man to their father. He had the same shaped face and deep-set eyes. But how could he be related? Suddenly there was a dull crunching sound and the young man was sprawled on the ground, looking up with shock on his face, blood running from his nose. Their father had hit him.

Siena gripped Serena's hand tight in shock at the sudden violence. Their father turned back and gestured angrily for them to follow him. The path was so narrow that they had to step over the young man's legs. Siena was too scared to look at him—he was so wild and feral.

They were ushered into the back of the car and Siena heard their father issue terse instructions to his men. Just then she heard the young man roar, 'I'm Rocco, your son—you bastard!'

When their father got into the car and it pulled away, Siena couldn't stop herself from looking behind them. She saw their father's men dragging the young man out of sight. She felt sick. Serena was looking stonily ahead but her hand gripped Siena's.

Their father caught Siena by the ear painfully and jerked her head round. Siena clamped her mouth shut. She knew better than to make a sound.

He forced her to look at him. 'What do you think you are doing?'

'Nothing, Papà.'

His mouth was a thin line of anger. 'Good, because you know what happens if you anger me.'

Serena's grip on Siena's hand was so tight she nearly cried out. Quickly Siena said, 'Yes, Papà.'

After a long, tense moment their father let her go and faced the front again. Siena knew very well what happened when she angered him. He would punish her sister Serena. It was never her. Always her sister. Because that was what amused him.

Siena didn't look at her sister, but they kept their hands tightly gripped together for the rest of the journey.

CHAPTER ONE

ANDREAS XENAKIS DIDN'T like the strength of the thrill of triumph that moved through him. It signified that this moment held more importance for him than he'd care to admit. Bitterly, he had to concede that perhaps it did. After all, practically within touching distance now was the woman who had all but cried *rape* for her own amusement, to protect her untarnished image in her father's eyes. She'd merited him a savage beating, losing his job, being blacklisted from every hotel in Europe and having to start over again on the other side of the world. Far away from anyone he'd known or who had known him.

She was still exquisite. More so. Andreas had found himself imagining that she couldn't possibly be as stunning as she'd been since he'd seen her five years ago. But she was. She was a woman now, not a teenager.

Her hair was so blonde it shone almost white under the soft lighting of a hundred chandeliers. It was pulled up into a high bun. She held herself with the same effortlessly regal bearing he'd first noticed in that glittering ballroom in Paris. His mouth compressed. She was a thoroughbred in the midst of lesser beings. He could see how women near her instinctively shut her out, as if sensing competition.

His eyes moved over the curve of her cheek and jaw. The patrician line of her nose more than hinted at the blue-blooded heritage of her Italian ancestry, diluted only in part by her half-

English mother who had been related to royalty. Her skin was still pale and looked soft: as soft as a rose petal. Andreas's belly clenched hard to recall just how soft it *had* felt under his fingers.

He'd touched her reverently, as if she were an ethereal goddess, and he'd felt as if he was marking her, staining her purity with his touch. His hands were fists by his sides now as he thought of how she'd urged him on with breathy, sexy entreaties in his ear: *'Please...I want you to touch me, Andreas.'* Only to turn on him almost in the same breath and accuse him of attacking her...

She turned then, to face towards him, and that low, simmering anger was eclipsed when blood rushed to his head and to his groin, making him simultaneously dizzy and hard.

He couldn't escape the impact of those huge, glittering bright blue eyes ringed with long dark lashes. But it was her mouth which drew his gaze and kept it. Sinfully lush and pink. Just waiting to be kissed...crushed under his. Andreas had to consciously will down the intense desire. He was fast being reduced to the instincts of an animal, and he hated her for having this effect on him. Still. *For ever*, mocked the small voice in his head.

No. Andreas rejected it fiercely. Not for ever. Just until he'd had her. Until they'd finished what she'd started when she'd upended his life so cruelly and comprehensively. Because she'd been curious and bored. Because she'd had the power. Because he'd been nothing.

Resolve firmed in Andreas's gut. He was far from nothing any more, and thanks to a cruel twist of circumstances Siena DePiero was reduced to lower than he'd ever been, rendering her exposed and vulnerable—to him.

Her blonde head dipped out of view momentarily and Andreas's insides contracted with something indefinable that went beyond where he wanted to investigate. He didn't like the fact that he was uncomfortably aware of other men's interest, of their gazes after her, covetous and even lascivious. It made him feel possessive and that was not welcome.

She'd had the gall to play with him once. Andreas desired her. That was all. His eyes caught sight of her bright blonde head again and he watched and waited as she drew ever closer to him in the crowd.

Siena DePiero was in the act of navigating through the crowd with a heavy tray, trying not to upend the contents over someone's feet, when a broad chest at her eye level stopped her from moving forward.

She looked up and had the impression of a very tall man, broad all the way through to his shoulders. A pristine tuxedo with a white bow-tie marked him out as slightly different. As Siena's mouth opened to say *excuse me* her gaze reached his face and her heart stopped.

He was no stranger.

Andreas Xenakis. Here.

The recognition was instantaneous. The knowledge was cataclysmic. It was as if mere minutes had passed since she'd last seen him, yet it had been five years. He looked bigger, darker, leaner.

She could instantly read the unmistakable light of cold hatred in his eyes and her insides contracted painfully. Of all the people to meet in this situation… No one would get more mileage out of it than Andreas Xenakis. And could she even blame him? a small voice mocked.

'Well, well, well.'

His voice was painfully familiar, immediately twisting her insides into a knot of tension.

'Fancy meeting you here.'

Siena could feel his eyes rake her up and down, taking in her server's uniform of white shirt, black tie and black trousers. The effect he had on her now was as devastating as it had been five years before. It was as if she had been plugged into an electrical socket and the current was running through her blood, making it hum, as disturbing and disconcerting as she remembered—especially in light of what had happened.

Her insides contracted even more painfully.

Dark slashing brows framed his incredible navy blue eyes. High cheekbones drew the eye down to a strong jaw. And his mouth…that beautiful sensuous mouth…was all at once sexy and mocking. He lifted one brow, clearly waiting for a response.

Struggling to retain some sense of composure, when she felt like a tiny boat being lashed on high seas, Siena managed to find her voice and said coolly, 'Mr Xenakis. How nice to see you again.'

His arched brow went higher and he let out a curt laugh. His voice wasn't so heavily accented any more. It had more of a mid-Atlantic twang. 'Even now you can make it sound as if you're greeting me at your own dinner party—not serving drinks to people you once wouldn't deign to look in the eye.'

Siena flinched minutely. She didn't have to be psychic to recognise that the man who stood before her now was a much harder and more ruthless creature than the man she'd met in Paris. Xenakis's meteoric rise to become one of the world's most prominent hoteliers at the ridiculously young age of thirty had been well documented in the press.

'I'm flattered you remember me,' he drawled, 'After all we've met only once—as memorable as that meeting was.'

He mocked her. Siena felt like pointing out pedantically that it had actually been twice. After all, she'd seen him again the morning after that catastrophic night. But *that* memory was far too much to handle right now.

'Yes.' She glanced away for a minute, uncomfortable under that dark gaze. 'Of course I remember you.'

Suddenly it was too much. The tray of glasses started to wobble alarmingly in Siena's hands as the full magnitude of seeing him again hit her. Surprising her, Andreas took it competently out of her white-knuckled grasp and put it down on a nearby table before she could object.

Just then they were interrupted by Siena's boss, who was shooting none too subtle daggers at Siena while smiling obsequiously at Andreas.

'Mr Xenakis, is everything all right here? If my staff have been in any way remiss—'

'No.' His voice was abrupt, cold. He truly was Lord of all he surveyed now. Exuding power and confidence and that tangible sexual charisma.

Feeling a little dizzy, Siena tuned back in to Xenakis's voice, being directed to her boss.

'Everything is fine. I am acquainted with Miss—'

Siena cut in urgently before Xenakis could say her hated name, 'Mr Xenakis, like I said, it was nice to see you again. If you'll excuse me, though, I really should get back to work.'

Siena picked up the heavy tray again and, without looking at Andreas Xenakis or her boss, fled on very shaky legs.

Andreas followed the progress of the bright blonde head, inordinately annoyed with this small rotund man for interrupting them. He was saying now, in a toadying voice, 'I'm so sorry about that, Mr Xenakis. Our staff have the strictest instructions not to make conversation with any of the guests, but Miss Mancini is new—'

Andreas bit out coldly, '*I* spoke to *her*, actually.' Then he realised something and looked at the man, 'You say her name is Mancini?'

'Yes,' her boss said absently, and then he smiled even more slimily, saying *sotto voce* to Andreas, 'Of course her looks are a bonus—she could be a model, if you ask me. I don't know what she's doing waitressing, but I can't complain. I've never had so many requests for her phone number.'

Andreas desisted from informing the man that she was waitressing because she was *persona non grata* in polite society across Europe. He pushed aside the fact of her name-change and felt something like rage building inside him. He fixed the manager with a look that would have felled many. 'I presume you do not give out her number, of course?'

The man immediately went puce and blustered, 'Well, I... Well, of course not, Mr Xenakis. I don't know what kind of a service you think I'm running here, but I can assure you—'

'Don't worry,' Andreas sliced in cuttingly. 'I *will* be assured once I've checked out your company thoroughly.'

With that he turned and walked in the direction he'd last seen Siena moving. He had something much more urgent to take his attention now: making sure Siena DePiero didn't disappear into thin air.

A couple of hours later Siena was walking quickly through the moonlit streets around Mayfair. She still hadn't fully processed that she'd seen Andreas Xenakis, here in London, where she'd come to hide and move on with her life. To her everlasting relief she hadn't bumped into him again, but she'd been horribly aware of his tall form and had endeavoured to make sure she stayed on the far side of the room at all times.

Now, as she walked and felt the blisters on her heels, she cursed herself for letting Andreas get to her like that. Yes, they had history. She winced inwardly. It wasn't a pretty history. She didn't want to be reminded of the blazing look of anger and betrayal on his face when she'd stood beside her father five years ago, holding her dress up over her chest, and agreed shakily: *'Yes, he attacked me, Papa. I couldn't stop him...'*

Andreas had cut in angrily, his Greek accent thick. 'That's a downright lie. She was begging me—'

Her father had held up an imperious hand and cut Andreas off. He'd turned to face Siena and she'd looked up at him, terrified of his power to inflict punishment if he chose to believe Andreas.

He'd said quietly, 'He's lying, isn't he? You would *never* let a man like this touch you, would you? Because you know you're infinitely better than him.'

Struggling to hide her disgust and hatred, Siena had given the only answer she could. She'd nodded and felt sick. 'Yes, he's lying. I would never allow someone like him to touch me.'

Thinking of the unpalatable past made Siena feel trembly and light-headed. She didn't want to contemplate the very uncomfortable fact that he still had such a profound effect on her.

Once again, though, she marvelled at how far removed he was from the man who had once presided over servers in a hotel. In all honesty she was surprised he'd recognised her at all from his lofty position. She knew how easy it was to see only the hand that served you, not the person. Siena recalled her father's blistering anger when he'd berated her once for aiding a waiter who'd dropped a tray at one of his legendary parties. He'd hauled her into his offce and gripped her arm painfully.

'Don't you know who we are? You step over people like him. You do *not* stop to help them.'

Siena had bitten back the angry retort on her lips. *Just like you stepped over your own illegitimate son in the street? Our own brother?* That audacious comment alone would have merited her sister a severe beating. That was his preferred twisted form of torture—if Siena provoked him, Serena would be punished.

Siena saw the bus stop in the distance and breathed a sigh of relief. Tomorrow she would have forgotten all about bad memories and running into Andreas Xenakis. Her insides lurched, mocking her assertion. For one second earlier, when she'd first seen Andreas, she'd imagined she was dreaming.

She'd never forgotten what she had done to that man by falsely accusing him. More often than she cared to admit she remembered that night and how, with just a look and a touch, he'd made her lose any sense of rationality and sanity. On some level, when she'd read about his stellar success in the newspapers, she'd been relieved; to see him flourishing far better than she would have ever expected assuaged some tiny part of the guilt she felt.

Resolutely Siena pushed down her incendiary thoughts. Familiar nagging anxiety took their place. She wondered now, as she approached the bus stop, if the two jobs she had would be enough to help her sister. But she knew with a leaden feeling that nothing short of a miracle could do that.

Siena had just arrived under the shelter of the bus stop when she noticed a sleek silver sports car pulling up alongside where she stood. Even before the electric window lowered on the passenger side Siena's heart-rate had increased.

The starkly handsome features of Andreas Xenakis looked out and Siena backed away instinctively. His presence was evidence that he wasn't about to let her off so easily. He wanted to torture her and make the most out of her changed circumstances. In a second he'd jumped out of the car and was lightly holding her elbow.

'Please.' He smiled urbanely, as if stopping to pick up women at bus stops resplendent in a tuxedo was entirely normal for him. 'Let me give you a lift.'

Siena was so tense she felt as if she might crack in two. Very aware of her ill-fitting thin denim jacket in the biting early spring breeze, and the fatigue that made her bones ache, she bit out, 'I'm fine, thank you. The bus will be along shortly.'

Andreas shook his head. He had that same incredulous expression that he'd worn when she'd spoken to him before. 'Are your co-workers aware you could probably have conversed with every foreign guest in that room in their own tongue?'

Hurt at this back-handed compliment, and his all too banal but accurate assessment of her misery Siena pulled her arm free. She acted instinctively, wanting to say something to prick his pride and hopefully push him away. 'I said I'm fine, thank you very much. I'm sure you have better things to do than follow me around like some besotted puppy dog.'

His eyes flashed dangerously at that, and Siena hated herself for those words. They reminded her of the poison that had dropped from her lips that night in Paris. They were the kind of words Andreas would expect her to say. But they weren't having the desired effect at all. She should have realised that he wasn't like other men—she remembered the way he'd stood up to her father with such innate pride. One of the very few people who hadn't cowered.

He merely looked even more dangerous now, and grabbed her arm again. 'Let's go, Signorina DePiero. The bus is coming and I'm blocking the lane.'

Siena looked past Andreas and saw the double-decker bus bearing down. A sharp blast of the horn made her flinch. She could see the others waiting at the bus stop shooting them dirty looks because their journey home was being held up.

Siena looked at Andreas and he said ominously, 'Don't test me, Siena. I'll leave the car there if I have to.'

Another blast of the horn had someone saying with irritation, 'Oh, just take the lift, will you? We want to get home.'

For a second Siena felt nothing but excoriating isolation. And then Andreas had led her to the car and was handing her into the low seat before shutting the door. He slid smoothly into the other side.

'Do up your belt,' he instructed curtly, before adding acidly, 'Or are you used to having even *that* done for you?'

His words cut through the fog of shock clouding her brain

and she fumbled to secure the belt with hands that were all fingers and thumbs.

She retaliated in a sharp voice. 'Don't be ridiculous.'

Andreas expertly negotiated the car into the stream of traffic. It was so smooth it felt as if they were gliding above the ground. It had been long months since Siena had been in such luxurious confines, and the soft leather seat moulded around her body, cupping it in a way that was almost sensual. Her hands curled into fists on her lap against the sensation and her jaw was taut.

She unclenched it. 'Stop the car and let me out, please. I can make my own way home. I got in purely to stop you causing a scene.'

'I've spent six months looking for you, Siena, so I'm not about to let you go that easily.'

Six months ago her father had disappeared, leaving his entire fortune in tatters, and leaving Siena and Serena to stand among the ashes and take the opprobrium that had come their way in their father's cowardly absence. Siena looked at Andreas with horror on her face and something much more ambiguous in her belly. Tonight *hadn't* been an awful coincidence?

Shakily she said, 'You've been looking for me?'

His mouth tightened and he confirmed it. 'Since the news of your father's disappearance and the collapse of your fortune.'

He glanced at her and she held herself tightly, wanting to shiver at the thought of his determination to find her again. To punish her? *Why else?* a small voice crowed.

Softly, lethally, he said, 'We have unfinished business, wouldn't you agree?'

Panic constricted Siena's throat. She wasn't ready for a reckoning with this man. 'No, I wouldn't. Now, why don't you just stop the car and let me out?'

Andreas ignored her entreaty and drawled easily, 'Your address, Siena…or we'll spend the night driving around London.'

Siena's jaw clenched again. She saw the way his long-fingered hand rested on the steering wheel. For all of his nonchalance she suddenly had the impression that he was actually far more intractable than her father had ever been. He'd certainly proved that he had a ruthless nose when it came to business.

Siena had on more than one occasion closeted herself in her father's study to follow Andreas's progress online. She'd read about him shutting down ailing hotels with impunity, his refusing to comment on rumours that he didn't care about putting hundreds out of work just to increase his own growing portfolio. In the same searches she'd seen acres of newsprint devoted to his love-life, which appeared to be hectic and peopled with only the most beautiful women in the world. Siena didn't like to admit how she'd noticed that they were all lustrous brunettes or redheads. Evidently blondes weren't his type any more.

Suspecting now that he would indeed drive around all night if she didn't tell him, Siena finally rapped out her address.

'See? That wasn't so hard, was it?'

Siena scowled and looked right ahead.

There was silence for a few minutes, thickening the tension, and then he said, 'So, where did you get Mancini from?'

Siena looked at him. 'How did you know?' Then she remembered and breathed out shakily. 'My boss must have mentioned it.'

'Well?' he asked, as if he had all the time in the world to wait for an answer.

Tightly, Siena eventually replied, 'It was my maternal grandmother's maiden name. I didn't want to risk anyone recognising me.'

'No,' the man beside her responded dryly, 'I can imagine why not.'

Anger at his insouciance, and the ease with which he'd just turned up to humiliate her, made Siena snap, 'You really shouldn't have followed me, you know.'

He replied all too easily. 'Look on it as a concerned friend merely wishing to see how you're doing.'

Siena snorted scathingly but her heart was thumping, '*Friend?* Somehow I doubt you've ever put yourself in that category where I'm concerned.' It was more likely to be a definite foe.

Andreas Xenakis shot her a look then, and Siena recoiled back in her seat. It was so…so carnal and censorious.

He growled softly, 'You're right. We were closer to lovers. And friends don't, after all, cry rape when it suits them to save face.'

Siena blanched. 'I *never* used that word.'

Andreas's jaw clenched hard. 'As good as. You accused me of attacking you when we both know that only seconds before your father arrived you were begging me to—'

'Stop!' cried Siena, her breathing becoming agitated.

She could remember all too well how it had felt to have Andreas Xenakis pressing her down into the chaise longue, the way she'd strained up towards him, aching for him to put his hands on her *everywhere*. And when he'd moved his hand up between her stockinged legs she'd parted them…tacitly telling him of her intense desire.

'Why?' Andreas drawled. 'You can't handle the truth? I thought you were made of sterner stuff, DePiero. You forget you showed your true colours that night.'

Siena turned her head and looked stonily out of the window. The truth was that she had no excuse for her reprehensible behaviour that night. She *had* begged Andreas to make love to her. She *had* kissed him back ardently. When he'd pulled her dress down to expose one breast she'd sighed with exquisite pleasure and he'd kissed her there.

The car pulled up to a set of traffic lights at that moment, and the urge to escape was sudden and instinctive. Siena went to open her door to jump out, but with lightning-fast accuracy Andreas's arm restrained her with a strength that was awesome. Long fingers wrapped around her slender arm, and the bunched muscle of his arm against her soft belly was a far more effective restraint than if he'd locked the doors. Her skin tightened over her bones, drawing in and becoming sensitised. Her breasts felt heavy and tight, her nipples stiffening against the material of her bra.

The car moved off again and Siena pushed his arm off her with all her strength. That brief touch was enough to hurtle her back in time all over again and she struggled to contain herself. The fact that he was so determined to toy with her like this was utterly humiliating.

He pulled up outside a discreetly elegant period apartment building on a wide quiet street. He'd hopped out of the car and was at her open door, holding out an expectant hand, before she knew what was happening.

Siena shrank back and looked up at him. 'This isn't where I live.' *It's a million miles from where I live,* she thought.

'I'm aware of that. However, it is where *I* live, and as we were passing I thought we'd stop so we can catch up on old times over a coffee.'

Siena held back a snort of derision and crossed her arms, looking straight ahead with a stony expression. 'I am not getting out of this car, Xenakis. Take me home.'

Andreas's voice was merely amused. 'First I couldn't get you into it and now I can't get you out of it. They say women are mercurial…'

Before she knew it Andreas had bent down to her level and reached in to undo her seat belt. Siena flapped at his hands in a panic until he stilled them with his. His face was very close to hers and Siena could feel her hair unravelling. She was breathing harshly. His scent teased her nostrils, exactly as she remembered it. Not changed. Oaky and musky and very male.

A voice came from behind Andreas. 'Mr Xenakis? Do you want me to park the car?'

Without taking his eyes off Siena's, Andreas answered, 'Yes, please, Tom. I'll be taking Ms DePiero home shortly, so keep it nearby.'

'Aye-aye, sir,' came the jaunty response.

Siena struggled for a few seconds against Andreas's superior strength and will. She saw the boy waiting behind him. Innate good manners and the fear of causing a scene that had been drummed into her since babyhood made her bite out with reluctance, 'Fine. One coffee.'

Andreas stood up, and this time Siena had no choice but to put her hand in his and let him help her out of the low-slung vehicle. To her chagrin he kept a tight hold of her hand as he tossed his keys to the boy and led her into the building, where a concierge held the door open in readiness.

Once in the hushed confines of the lift Siena tried to pull her hand back, but Andreas was lifting it to inspect it. He opened out her palm and his touch made some kind of dangerous lethargy roll through her, but she winced when she followed his gaze. Her palm sported red chafed skin, calluses. Proof of her very new working life.

He turned it over and Siena winced even more to see him inspecting her bitten nails—the resurgence of a bad habit she'd had for a short time in her teens, which had been quickly overcome when her father had meted out a suitable punishment on Serena, her sister.

Her hands were a far cry from the soft lily-white manicured specimens they'd used to be. Exerting more effort this time, and knowing that she'd just been cured of her nail-biting habit once again, she finally pulled free of Andreas's grip and said mulishly, 'Don't touch me.'

With a rough quality to his voice that resonated inside her, Andreas asked, 'How did they get like this from waitresssing?'

Siena fought against the pull of something that felt very vulnerable. 'I'm not just waitressing. I'm working as a cleaner in a hotel by day too.'

Andreas tipped up her chin and inspected her face, touched under her eyes where she knew she sported dark shadows. That vulnerability was blooming inside her, and for a second Siena thought she might burst into tears. To counteract it—and the ease with which this man seemed to be able to push her buttons—she said waspishly, 'Feeling sorry for the poor little rich girl, Andreas?'

At that moment the lift bell pinged and the doors opened silently. Siena and Andreas were locked in some kind of silent combat. Andreas's eyes went dark, their blue depths becoming distinctly icy as he took his fingers away from her face and smiled.

'Not for a second, Siena DePiero. You forget that I've seen you in action. A piranha would be more vulnerable than you.'

Siena couldn't believe the dart of hurt that lanced her at his words, and was almost glad when he turned. With his hand on her elbow, he led her out of the lift and into a luxuriously carpeted corridor decked out in smoky grey colours with soft lamps burning on a couple of tables.

The one door indicated that Andreas had no neighbours to disturb him, and Siena guessed this must be the penthouse apartment in the building. The lift doors closed behind them and then Andreas was opening the door and standing aside to allow Siena to precede him into his apartment. Only his assurance to the car park valet that he would be taking her home shortly gave Siena the confidence to go forward.

She rounded on him as he closed the door and blurted out belatedly, 'Don't call me DePiero. My name is Mancini now.'

After a long second Andreas inclined his head and drawled, with a hint of dark humour, 'I'll call you whatever you like…'

Stifling a sound of irritation, Siena backed away and turned around again, facing into the main drawing room. Her eyes widened. She'd grown up in the lap of luxury, but the sheer understated level of elegance in Andreas's apartment took her breath away. She'd been used to seeing nothing but *palazzos* laden down with antiques and heavy paintings, everything gold-plated, carpets so old and musty that dust motes danced in the air when you moved…but this was clean and sleek.

Siena only became aware that she had advanced into the drawing room and was looking around with unabashed curiosity when she saw Andreas standing watching her with his hands in his pockets. The sheer magnificence of the man in his tuxedo shocked her anew and she flushed, wrapping her arms around herself in an unconscious gesture of defence.

Andreas shook his head and smiled wryly before walking towards a sideboard which held several bottles of drink and glasses. He said now, with his back to Siena, 'You really know how to turn it on, don't you?'

Siena tensed. 'Turn what on?'

He turned around, a bottle of something in his hand, eyes gleaming in the soft light. 'It must be automatic after years of acting the part of innocent virginal heiress…'

When Siena was stubbornly silent, because he had no idea how close to the truth he skated, Andreas gestured half impatiently and clarified, 'That air of vulnerability, and looking as though butter wouldn't melt in your mouth.'

Hating herself for being so transparent, and hating him for misjudging her so comprehensively while knowing she couldn't very well blame him for his judgement, Siena schooled her expression. She carefully uncrossed her arms and shrugged one shoulder negligently. 'What can I say? You have me all figured out, Mr Xenakis.'

He poured a dark liquid into two glasses and came over, holding one out. 'I know I offered you a coffee, but try this. It's a very fine port. And you didn't have a problem using my name when we first met. Mr Xenakis is so...*formal.* Please, call me Andreas.'

Siena took the glass he offered, suddenly glad of something to hold onto—anything to will down the memory of how she had used his name before, *'Andreas, please kiss me...'*

He gestured to the comfortable-looking couch and chairs arranged around a low coffee table which held huge books of photographs that looked well thumbed. 'Please, take a seat, Siena. Make yourself comfortable.'

Siena was torn for a moment between wanting to demand he take her home and curling up in the nearest chair so she could sleep for a week.

A little perturbed by how weak she suddenly felt, she went and sat down in the nearest chair. Andreas sat on the couch to her left, his long legs stretched out and disturbingly close to her feet, which she pulled primly close to her chair.

He smiled and it was dangerous.

'Still afraid you might catch some social disease from me, Siena?'

CHAPTER TWO

'DON'T BE SILLY,' Siena replied quickly, humiliated when she thought of what had happened, of the vile untruths she'd uttered and all to protect her sister.

When she thought of how innocently she'd wanted him that night in Paris and how it had all gone so horribly wrong she felt nauseous. This man hated her. It vibrated on the air between them and Siena had the very futile sense that even if she tried to defend herself and tell him what her reasons had been for acting so cruelly he'd laugh until he cried. He looked so impervious now. Remote.

Andreas sat forward, the small glass cradled between long fingers. 'Tell me, why did you leave Italy?'

Siena welcomed this diversion away from dangerous feelings and looked at him incredulously, wondering how he could even ask that question. She hated the familiar burn of humiliation that rose up inside her when she thought of the odious charges that had been levelled at her father after his business had imploded in on itself, revealing that he'd been juggling massive debts for years and that everything they possessed, including his precious family *palazzo* in Florence, was owned by the banks.

Her mouth twisted. 'As you can imagine, the price on myself and my sister's heads fell dramatically when it became apparent that we'd lost our fortune. I'm sure I don't need to tell you that we became *personae non grata* overnight.'

Andreas's eyes narrowed. 'No. It would be untruthful of me not to admit that I knew your father had been soliciting prostitutes for years, and about the evidence of his involvement in drugs and political corruption. But proof that he'd been trafficking women all over Europe for sex must have been the killer blow for two penniless heiresses. No one wants to be seen to be associating with a scandal of that level.'

The shame Siena felt nearly strangled her. Her father had solicited prostitutes while married to their mother because it had excited him. He'd fathered a son with one of those women. She'd thought she'd hated her father before…but she'd hated him even more when he'd disappeared into thin air to avoid the numerous charges levelled against him. To this day no one knew where he was, and Siena never wanted to see him again.

The thought of all those poor defenceless and vulnerable women being sold into a life of torture and degradation… Even now bile rose in her throat, because it had also been proved that her father had been more than just involved in a peripheral sense. He'd been an active participant.

Andreas must have seen something in her expression and he said quietly. 'Your father's sins are not your sins.'

Siena was taken aback at this assertion. She looked at him, unable to read his face. 'Perhaps not, but people don't want to believe that.'

'Did the press in Italy gave you a hard time?' He answered her disbelieving look with a shrug. 'I was travelling in South America for work when the full extent of your father's scandal hit. By the time I got back to Europe your father had disappeared and a new scandal was unfolding. I missed most of it.'

Siena thought of the relentless days of headlines like: *Heiresses no more. Who will marry the poor little rich girls now?* And: *Serena DePiero caught in flagrante just days after dis-*

graced father's disappearance! That had been the moment Siena had known she had to get herself and Serena out of Italy. Her sister had been spiralling dangerously out of control, and she'd been barely clinging onto sanity after everything they'd known had been ripped asunder.

Siena hadn't expected any quarter from the press—she'd seen how they delighted in savaging the once lofty and un-touchable of society—and thanks to her father's extreme hu-bris the DePieros had had it coming. Nevertheless she voiced an understatement in a flat voice. 'Yes, you could say they gave us a hard time.'

Andreas was surprised at the lack of emotion in Siena's voice. The lack of reproach or injury. He could well imagine the field-day the press had had at seeing two blonde and blue-eyed princesses reduced to nothing.

Once again he had to marvel at her sheer natural beauty. She wore not a scrap of make-up but her skin glowed like a pearl. In this world of artifice and excess she really was a rare jewel. Even in the plain shirt and tie, that threadbare denim jacket, he could see the tantalising curves of her body. Fuller now that she was a woman, not a teenager.

Desire was hot and immediate, tightening his body. A fit of pique went through Andreas when he realised that he'd sub-consciously avoided blonde women in the last five years, seek-ing out the complete opposite and telling himself that she'd burned his taste for blondes. But she hadn't. He just hadn't wanted any blonde except *her*.

Women didn't usually reduce him to such immediate car-nal reaction, no matter how desirable or beautiful. And yet she had from the very first moment he'd laid eyes on her…

Andreas looked at her now with fresh resolve filling his belly and lifted his glass. 'To whatever the future might bring.'

Siena had a very scary suspicion that the future Andreas was envisaging had something to do with *her*. Very deliberately she ignored his toast and drained her glass, put it down on the nearby table. The alcohol blazed its way down her throat.

Andreas looked merely amused and chided softly, 'A 1977 port should be savoured a little more delicately than that, but each to their own.'

He downed his too. Siena blanched. She could just imagine how much it had cost. Her father had thought of himself as an expert in fine wines so she'd learnt something by proxy.

Thinking of her father made her think of her sister, and that made her stand up jerkily, only vaguely aware of the stunning view of London on the other side of the huge windows. 'I really do need to get home. I have an early start in the morning.'

Andreas rose too, as fluidly as a panther, rippling sinew and muscle very evident despite the severe cut of his suit. As if it barely contained him. Siena would have taken a step back, but the chair was behind her.

She sensed a spiking of electricity in the air and there was a pregnant pause just before he said innocuously, 'Very well.'

He went to a discreet phone on the sideboard and picked it up, saying to someone, 'I'm coming back down. Please have my car brought round. Thank you.'

He extended his arm to allow her to precede him from the room, and to Siena's utter chagrin her overwhelming feeling wasn't one of relief. She was a little confused. She'd expected…*more*. More of a fight? And yet he was happy to let her go so easily. Something bitter pierced her. Perhaps he'd just wanted to amuse himself by seeing the disgraced heiress up close and he was already bored.

So why did she feel so desolate all of a sudden?

Andreas stepped into the lift behind Siena and pressed the button. He might be giving her the illusion of letting her go, but that was not his intention in the slightest. Seeing her again had merely solidified his desire to have her in his bed. Finally.

Acquiescent and *his*. That disdain she did so well would have no place in the relationship they would have. She was in no position to argue or resist him, and the thought of seeing her come undone was heady in the extreme.

His car was waiting by the kerb and a young security guard jumped out, giving the keys to Andreas, who held the passenger door open for Siena to get in.

Siena stood stiffly by the open door and looked at Andreas without meeting his eye. She was still trembling at the way his hand had rested lightly on the small of her back the whole way down in the elevator. And also at the speed with which he now appeared to want to get rid of her.

'If you can point me in the direction of the nearest tube I'll make my own way home.'

Andreas's voice was like steel. 'It's almost eleven-thirty at night. There is no way you're taking the tube alone. Get into the car, Siena, or I will put you in myself. Don't think I won't.'

Siena looked at him properly and saw how stern he seemed. She felt a shiver of something go through her—recognition of how huge and broad he was against the night sky. And yet she wasn't scared of him. Not as she'd been of her father. She somehow knew instinctively that Andreas would never lash out like that. Violence towards women was born of weakness and fear. Andreas didn't have that in him. And it surprised her to admit that she trusted this gut feeling so much.

Knowing that if she walked off now he'd just follow her again, Siena gave in and slid into the car, its luxurious confines once again surrounding her like a cocoon. Until Andreas got in beside her and the atmosphere turned from relaxing to electric.

As they pulled away from the kerb Andreas asked easily, 'Did your sister come to London with you?'

Instantly Siena tensed. She answered carefully, 'No… She went to…to the south of France to stay with friends of hers.'

Andreas glanced at Siena, who was looking stonily ahead.

He had to concede that she'd never taken after her more obvious sister by appearing in the gossip columns. Siena clearly preferred to clean toilets rather than to be seen in polite society again and be exposed to ridicule or censure.

He had to admit to a grudging and surprising respect that Siena was doing the sort of work she would have taken completely for granted her whole life. Perhaps now that their father was gone Siena saw no need to be responsible for the precious family name and was happy to wash her hands of her infamous sister, who had been well known as a party girl.

In truth, Andreas didn't really care about Serena. The sister he was concerned about was sitting right beside him, her legs looking very long as she angled them well away from him. He allowed himself a small predatory smile to think of a time when they would be wrapped around his hips as he finally exorcised this demon from his blood for good.

He hadn't elaborated on the fact that he had been actively looking for her for six months. In fact he'd been thinking about her ever since Paris. However, it had only been six months ago, when he'd finally had the luxury of time after establishing himself, that he'd begun to focus on such a personal pursuit. Siena DePiero had always been in his sights...

To Siena's relief Andreas seemed to be done with questioning her, and they drove in silence through the empty London streets. Rain started to spatter gently on the windscreen. For the first time since she'd left Italy Siena felt a pang of homesickness and it surprised her. She'd left Italy never wanting to see it again.

She'd spent many a night looking out of her window dreaming of another life—one without constrictions and pain and tension and always the unbearable pressure to act a certain way. She'd dreamed of a life full of love and affection. The only affection she'd really known had come from her sister— her poor, damaged sister. Their mother had died when they were both small girls. Siena had only the vaguest memories of a fragrant blonde woman who'd used to come into their room at night dressed in glittering finery.

She realised that they were close to her street already, and she directed Andreas into the labyrinth of smaller streets that led to her home. He pulled to a stop and looked out incredulously at the bleak, lonesome apartment block standing on wasteground.

'You're living *here?*'

Defensively Siena said, 'It's near the tube and the bus.'

Andreas was shaking his head in disbelief. He undid his seat belt and got out. Siena noticed that he'd taken an umbrella from somewhere and was holding it up now, as he came to her door and opened it.

She got out and the wind whipped around her, tugging her hair out of its bun completely. Feeling flustered, she said, 'Look, thanks for the lift...'

She moved to walk around Andreas and go into the flats, but stopped when Andreas kept pace beside her. She looked at him. 'Where do you think you're going?'

He was grim. 'I'm walking you to your apartment. You are *not* going in there alone.'

A new sense of pride stiffened Siena's backbone. 'I've been living here alone for months now and I've been fine. I can assure you that—'

Andreas wasn't listening. He'd taken her elbow in his hand and was guiding her across the litter-strewn ground. Irritation raced up Siena's spine. This was exactly what her father had used to do.

Once inside the main door, which hung haphazardly on broken hinges, and under the unforgiving flourescent lights, Siena pulled free, 'This is fine.'

Andreas was folding down the umbrella, though, and then he spotted a sullen youth lurking in a corner. He called the boy over and handed him a folded note and the umbrella. 'Keep an eye on the car for me?' he said.

The boy looked at the money and went white, then looked back to Andreas and nodded his head vigorously.

He took the umbrella before speeding off to stand guard.

Siena didn't like how the tiny gesture of Andreas giving him the umbrella made her feel soft inside. Churlishly she said, 'It'll be up on blocks by the time you leave.'

'O, ye of little faith,' Andreas murmured, and hit the elevator button.

Siena watched as he grew impatient when the lift didn't materialise straight away, and stood back to point at the stained concrete stairs. 'It's a cliché, I know, but the lift isn't working—and I'm all the way up on the fourteenth floor.' She couldn't quite keep the satisfaction out of her voice.

The light of determination was a definite glint in Andreas's eye as he said, 'Lead the way.'

Siena was huffing and puffing by floor ten, and very aware of Andreas right behind her. When they finally reached the door to her flat she turned to face him. She felt hot, and the hair on the back of her neck felt damp with perspiration. Her heart was hammering.

'Thank you. This is me.'

Andreas barely had a hair out of place, and not so much as a hint of the effort of climbing up fourteen sets of hard concrete stairs. Although somewhere along the way he had tugged his bow-tie loose, and the top button of his shirt was open, revealing the top of his olive-skinned chest and some springy dark hair.

Siena's belly clenched hard. She could remember impatiently undoing his shirt buttons that night in Paris, ripping his tie open…

Andreas was looking around the bare corridor. Someone

was shouting in a nearby flat and then something smashed against a door, making Siena flinch.

Andreas cursed and took the keys out of her numb fingers. 'Let's get you inside.'

He was doing it again. Taking command, all but pushing her through the door into a bare and forlorn-looking space filled with stained carpet. Siena had done her best to get rid of the stains, with little success. She only hoped that they weren't what she thought they were…

Siena put on her one small lamp and regretted it as soon as she did so, because it sent out a far too seductive pink and warm glow. Feeling thoroughly threatened now, she put out her hand for her keys and snapped, 'You've seen me safely in—now, please leave.'

Looking supremely at ease, Andreas just shut the door behind him and said softly, 'This must be hard for you…'

Siena went very still and her hand dropped to her side. He had no idea…how *easy* this had been for her. To leave behind the tainted trappings of suffocating wealth and excess had been a relief. But that was something no one would ever understand. She'd certainly never be explaining it to *this* man, who had grabbed onto success and wealth with both hands and was thoroughly enjoying it. And could she begrudge him that? Even if his methods were dubious? Of course not. She had given up that right five years before.

She put her hand out again for her keys. 'I have to be up early for work.'

Andreas didn't move. He just looked at her, those dark, unreadable eyes roving over her face and over her hair, which was tumbled around her shoulders now, making Siena want to drag it back, tie it up.

Feeling desperate, she said, *'Please.'*

'But what if you didn't have to get up early?'

Siena blinked at Andreas, not understanding him. She

shook her head. 'What do you mean? I start work at six-thirty a.m. It takes me an hour to get there...'

Andreas's face was so starkly beautiful in the dim light that she could feel herself being hypnotised. Much as she had been when she'd stood in front of him in that hotel boutique shop, in that dress. She'd taken it off after that night and thrown it in the bin, unable to look at it and not feel sickened.

He said now in a silky tone, 'What I mean is that you have a choice, Siena... I'd like to offer you an alternative.'

It took a second...but then his words sank in along with the very explicit look in his eyes. Since she'd been in England other men had posed much the same question—like the man who had come back to get something from his hotel room and found her making his bed. Except what he'd been offering had been stated in much cruder terms.

Shame and something much hotter curled through her belly, making self-disgust rise. She took a sidestep back and injected as much icy disdain as she could into her voice. 'If you're suggesting what I think you're suggesting then clearly you refuse to believe that I want you to leave me alone.'

Andreas took a step closer and panic spiked in Siena, making her take another step back. She felt out of her depth and unbelievably vulnerable. All of the familiar surroundings of her old life were gone. The part she'd played had been as good as scripted. Now she was utterly defenceless, and the one man in the world who hated her guts was propositioning her. And she hated that it didn't disgust her the way it should.

He reached out to trail a finger down one cheek, across her jawbone and down to where the pulse beat hectically under her skin at her throat. 'Even now you affect disgust, but your body betrays you. What happened in Paris...you were as involved as I was—as hot and eager as anything I've ever seen. And yet you didn't hesitate to shift the blame to me to keep yourself pure in your father's bigoted eyes. God forbid the untouchable heiress had been rolling around on a chair with a mere hotel employee.'

Siena slapped his hand away and stepped back, hating how breathy she sounded. 'Get out of here now, Xenakis. Rehashing the past is of no use.'

The anger Andreas had been keeping in check spilled over into his voice. 'You can't bring yourself to offer up even the most grudging of apologies, can you? Even now, when you don't have a cent to your name or a reputation to safeguard.'

Shame gripped Siena—and guilt. Ineffectually she said, 'I…am…sorry.'

Derision laced Andreas's voice as he sneered, 'Spare me the insincere apology when it's all but dragged from you.'

His face was suddenly etched with self-disgust, and he half turned from Siena, raking his hair with a hand. She had a vivid memory of seeing him the following morning, shocked at his black eye and swollen jaw. Evidence of her father's men's dirty work. She'd tried to apologise then, but hadn't been able to speak over his very justified wrath.

Contrition and a stark desire to assure him that she *was* truly sorry made her reach out impulsively to touch his sleeve. She dropped her hand hurriedly when he looked at her suspiciously. She gulped under his almost black gaze and said truthfully, 'I never intended to…to lie about what happened. Or that you should lose your job.'

Andreas smiled, but it was harsh. 'No, possibly you didn't. You would have had your fun with me on the chaise longue of that boutique and then you would have gone on your way, with another notch on your busy bedpost. You forget that I know exactly what you girls were like: avaricious, bored and voracious. But you hadn't counted on Papà finding you *in flagrante delicto,* and you made sure that he would not suspect his precious daughter had such base desires. It was much easier to accuse a poor Greek hotel employee.'

Siena blanched. That was exactly what she had done. But not for *her* survival, for her sister's. That was something she could never imagine explaining to this intractable, vengeful man. Especially not when Serena was still so vulnerable. And not when Siena was still reeling with the effect he had on *her*.

Andreas slashed his hand through the air and said curtly, 'You're right, though. Rehashing the past is of no use.'

Those dark blue eyes narrowed on Siena again, with a renewed gleam of something that looked suspiciously like determination.

'Are you really telling me you're so proud that you relish living like this?' His voice became cajoling. 'Don't you miss sleeping until lunchtime and having nothing to worry about other than what time you've scheduled your beauty appointments or which dress you'll wear that evening?' He continued relentlessly. 'Are you really expecting me to believe that you wouldn't have all that back if you could? That you wouldn't seize the opportunity to walk amongst your peers again?'

Siena felt sick. The thought of allowing this man to get any closer, where he could possibly discover the vulnerability hidden deep inside her, made her break out in a cold sweat. He thought she had the wherewithal to handle him, that it would be second nature, when she didn't have the first clue about handling a man like him.

She pushed aside the fact that her apology had been as futile as she'd believed it would be and tossed her head in her most haughty fashion, eyes flashing. 'I would prefer to clean your toilets rather than do as you're suggesting. Perhaps you think that because I'm desperate I'll say yes to becoming your mistress. Is that it, Xenakis?'

Andreas smiled and bared his teeth. 'I thought I told you to call me Andreas—and, yes, I think you'll agree because you miss your life of luxury. But, more than that, because despite everything you want me...'

Siena went cold. She did want him, but he had no clue who she really was, or why she'd had to betray him so awfully. He had no idea about the tender beating inner heart of her that had very fragile hopes and dreams for a life far from the one she knew. He only saw a spoilt ruined heiress and a way to humiliate her. Because she'd rejected him. He had no idea who she'd had to protect, and that *that* was why she'd let him be accused in the worst way possible. She'd had no choice.

She knew now that, if given a chance, this man would take her and humiliate her for his own pleasure. For revenge.

In her most cutting voice Siena said, 'Contrary to your over-inflated view of your own levels of attraction, I *do not* want you. I may well be in a desperate situation *Mr Xenakis,* but I still have my pride and I wouldn't become your mistress for your sick amusement if you were the last man on this earth.'

Andreas looked at the woman standing just a few feet away from him and felt like clapping. Her clothes were crumpled and stained, her hair was tumbled around her face and shoulders in messy golden abandon, but she could have been a queen berating a lowly subject. And he wanted her with a hunger bordering on the very word she'd used herself: *desperation.*

He growled, 'I'm not in the habit of propositioning women who don't want me, Siena.'

She backed away at that, and reiterated with not a little desperation, 'I *don't* want you.'

'Liar.'

She saw the danger in Andreas's eyes. He advanced on her and she backed away, panic constricting her vocal cords, stopping her from saying anything. Panic at the awful, traitorous way her body was already getting hot, tingling with anticipation. If he kissed her now… Her mind blanked at the thought.

'Once again you're just too proud to admit you want me, Siena DePiero, and I'm going to prove how much you want me right now.'

It was insulting how easily Andreas was able to gather her into his arms and pull her close. From somewhere deep inside Siena dredged up the fight she needed. This man was far too dangerous to her. When he pulled her even closer and his head started to descend Siena acted on a visceral reflex to protect herself. She stiffened in his arms and lifted a hand to try and block his mouth from touching her. He obviously misread her intention and caught her wrist with lightning-fast reflexes. The strength of his grip made her gasp.

'Oh, no, you don't.'

Siena protested, 'But I wasn't—'

'No?' Andreas's mouth was hard.

He didn't believe her. Siena had never hit anyone in her life, and she felt sick at the thought that he could believe her capable of such violence.

'I wouldn't have hit you…' she whispered, willing him to believe her, staring directly into fathomless deep blue eyes.

Andreas's expression was stern. 'And you won't ever get the chance.' The threat in his voice was a very sensual one.

He kept her close with one arm secure around her waist and let her wrist go to bring his other hand up to cup her jaw with surprising gentleness, considering what he'd believed her about to do. And then, before she could make another move, Andreas angled his head down and his mouth closed over hers.

Shock rendered Siena helpless against the sensual attack Andreas administered. His mouth moved over hers with a confidence that was heady, eliciting an immediate response from Siena that she wasn't even aware of giving.

He was the only man who'd kissed her like this and she'd gone up in flames the first time. Nothing had changed. Heat pooled in her lower belly and spread slowly outwards, incinerating everything in its path. Her breasts tightened and felt heavy, achy. His arms around her were like a steel cage, but it was one she was pathetically loath to escape.

Siena was drowning in the scent of musky male, dimly aware of Andreas's hand moving down her jaw, caressing, and his fingers undoing the tie at the throat of her shirt, opening the top buttons.

His tongue teased her lips, making her strain to get closer, to allow him access so that he could stroke his tongue along hers. This was the headiest of illicit pleasures...

Unbeknownst to Siena, her hands had unfurled from the fists they'd been against Andreas's chest and were now spread out wide. She was up on tiptoe, as if to get closer to him. Andreas's hand cupped the back of her head, fingers tangled in long, silky blonde strands of hair. His other hand gripped her hip, kneading the flesh, making Siena move against him.

It was only when she felt air touch the exposed flesh of her neck and throat that Siena came to her senses and pulled back. She looked up, completely dazed, into dark blue eyes. Heavy-lidded and explicitly sexual.

Slowly realisation came over her like a chill wind, making all that heady sensuality wither away. One touch and she'd become a slave to her senses. Unable to rationalise anything.

Siena used her hands to push back violently, almost falling over in the process.

A million and one things were clamouring in her head, but worst of all was that she'd spectacularly—in neon lights and with fireworks—humiliated herself. She winced when she recalled her haughty tones—*I don't want you.*' And what had she just been doing? Proving herself a liar *again*.

She grasped at her open shirt and couldn't look Andreas in the eye. 'I'd like you to leave now.' Her voice sounded rusty and raw to her ears.

CHAPTER THREE

ANDREAS LOOKED AT Siena, holding onto her open shirt, looking almost shell-shocked, pale as the moonlight outside. His chest felt tight. This reaction was not something he'd expected. And then he realised: acting was second nature to this woman. It was in her blood—that made *his* blood boil. To have been duped again, even for a nanosecond…

His voice was harsh. 'There's no one here to cry wolf to now, Siena. You have to take responsibility for your actions.'

He started forward and suddenly her head came up. Her blue eyes were once again sparkling like jewels, her chin determined. Andreas stopped, his body still throbbing with heat. But he forced it back. Something hardened inside him. To think that for a second that he'd seen some kind of vulnerability…? Ludicrous.

He forced himself to be civilised when he felt anything but. 'You still want me, Siena, and you can deny it all you want but it's a lie. I am not leaving here without you tonight. You'll pay for what you did: *in my bed.*'

Siena opened her mouth and shut it again, shock pouring into her body. He sounded so utterly determined. As if he was prepared to carry her bodily from this place. Siena's mind skittered away from that all too disturbing scenario to think of his other assertion. How could she deny she wanted him after that little display of complete lack of control? His words terrified her, though—his easy assumption that she would just *go with him*. Just as her father had always expected her to do his bidding.

She'd tasted personal freedom for the first time since their father had disappeared and it terrified her to think of someone dictating her every move again.

Siena dropped her hand from her open top buttons and lifted her chin. 'You seriously think that I'll just walk out of here with you? How unbelievably arrogant *are* you?'

Andreas's eyes darkened ominously. 'I paid a high price for your petulant need to save face with your father that night, Siena. I was sacked and blacklisted from every hotel in Europe overnight, and I had the very unsavoury rumour of my having forced myself on a woman dogging my heels. My fledgling career was ruined. I had to go to America to start again.'

Siena couldn't bear to feel that shame again and she lashed out. 'So—what? I pay you now by becoming your mistress?'

Andreas smiled and it was feral. 'That and more, Siena De-Piero. You pay me by admitting to yourself *and me* just how much you want me.'

She looked at this man in the soft light of her grotty flat. He was standing like a maurauding pirate, legs firmly planted wide apart. Chest broad and powerful. Strip away the civilised veneer of the tuxedo and this man was a pure urban animal of the most potent kind.

He's been looking for you for six months. He's not just going to walk away... The realisation sent tendrils of panic mixed with something much more humiliatingly exciting through Siena's blood. The confines of the tiny flat seemed to draw in around them even more.

She emitted a curt laugh to hide her trepidation. 'So— what? You'd lock me into your penthouse apartment and take me out like a toy of some kind for your pleasure only?' She'd been aiming to sound scathing but her voice betrayed her, sounding almost as if she was considering this.

Andreas's eyes gleamed in the dim light and he smiled. 'I can't deny that that image does have its appeal, but, no, I'd have no problem being seen with you in public. *I* don't have an issue with public opinion—unlike some people.'

Andreas was looking at her coolly, clearly waiting for her to say something.

'And what then?' she asked, feeling a little hysterical at being in this situation, discussing this with Andreas Xenakis. 'You just drop me back here at the side of the road when you're done?'

Andreas's mouth firmed. 'I take care of all my...lovers.' He shrugged negligently. 'They're usually self-sufficient, but with your range of language skills alone I don't doubt that with a little help you could find a decent job...certainly something better than menial labour.'

Siena laughed. The hysteria was taking over. Controlling herself with an effort, she looked at Andreas. 'This truly is a turn-up for the books, isn't it? *You* offering to help *me* find a job...'

Siena's cutting voice was hiding one of her deepest vulnerabilities: the fact that she had no qualification beyond her exclusive education. Yes, she had numerous languages and could speak them fluently. Yes, she knew how to host a dinner party for fifty people and more. Yes, she knew how to arrange flowers and how to behave in front of royalty and diplomats, how to conduct conversation ranging from world politics to the history of art... But when it came to the real world—real life—she knew nothing. Had no skills or qualifications. She'd been destined for a life of social politics. And Andreas knew that.

She prayed he wouldn't touch her again and moved around him on wobbly legs to open the front door. There were no more disturbing sounds coming from her neighbours. She looked back into the room with relief, to see that Andreas had followed her. But the relief was short-lived when he gently but firmly pushed the door shut again.

Sounding eminently reasonable, Andreas said, 'I'm offering you an opportunity, Siena, a chance to move upwards and make a life for yourself again.'

Siena crossed her arms against this threat. He wasn't moving. She forced herself to look up at him. Her mouth twisted and she spoke her fears. 'We both know it's not an *offer,* Andreas. You haven't spent six months searching for me to just walk away.'

He smiled again and agreed equably, 'No, I haven't. It really wouldn't be such a chore, Siena… I'd see to it that you enjoyed yourself. You'd want for nothing.'

'For as long as your interest lasts?'

His face immediately became more stark and Siena knew she'd hit a nerve. She was intrigued despite herself. 'That's all I'm offering, Siena. A finite amount of time as my lover until we're both ready to move on. I have no desire for anything more permanent—certainly not with you.'

Siena barely registered his insult. She was fighting against his dark pull and she opened the door again—only to have Andreas reach out lazily and shut it. She wanted to stamp her feet and glared at him.

'Look, Xenakis—'

'No!'

His voice stopped the breath in her throat. He looked fierce and magnificent in the gloom. He came closer and her heart thudded painfully.

'*You* look. This is only going to end one way: by you agreeing to come with me now. If you want a further demonstration of how susceptible you are to me then by all means I'm happy to provide it here and now, but—' He cut himself off and looked around the room with clear disgust, then back to Siena. 'I personally would prefer to make love to you for the first time in more…luxurious surroundings.'

The thought and, worse, the knowledge that he could take her here if he so wanted made Siena move further away. She felt as if a noose was tightening around her neck.

Andreas watched as Siena distanced herself and curbed the almost animalistic urge he had to put her over his shoulder and carry her bodily out of this pathetic, stinking place. His blood was boiling with lust and determination. As soon as his mouth had touched hers he'd known with a visceral certainty that he would *not* be leaving her behind in this place. He didn't like to admit that a part of him couldn't bear to think of her in these surroundings. It was like dropping a perfect diamond into the filthiest of stagnant ponds.

Trying to curb the impatience he felt, Andreas pointed out, 'You don't have anyone to turn to, Siena. If you're hoping for some blue-blooded knight to ride up on a white horse and forgive you the sins of your father it's not going to happen. Don't forget—I *know* your sins.'

Siena turned to face Andreas again, hugging her arms even tighter around herself, unaware of how huge her eyes looked in her face.

His words had cut her far deeper than she wanted him to see. He was right. She didn't have anyone to turn to. She and Serena did have an older half-brother, but she had little doubt that after the treatment he'd received at the hands of their father, not to mention the way Siena and her sister had ignored him so blatantly when they'd seen him in the street the day he'd confronted their father, he would not relish her getting in touch out of the blue. He had become a billionaire financier against all the odds and must despise her just as he must despise their father, for humiliating him like a dog in the street.

Her sister was in no position to be of any support and never really had been, despite being the older by two years. And that brought Siena back to the stark realisation that *she* might have no one to turn to, but Serena was expecting to turn to Siena when she needed her. And she needed her now. Dismay filled her. How could she have forgotten even for a moment about Serena?

The hectic pulse of her blood mocked her. The reason was standing just feet away from her. Siena could feel the fight draining from her weary body. A sense of inevitability washed over her. It had been no coincidence that Andreas had met her tonight. He'd *searched* for her. And he would not rest now he knew where she was. She had nowhere else to go. Nowhere to hide. No resources.

As if he sensed the direction her thoughts were taking, Siena could see Andreas's eyes flash triumphantly in the gloom.

Suddenly, as if she'd been injected with a dose of adrenalin, her brain became clear. Thinking of her sister focused her thoughts. *If* she was going to walk out of this apartment with this man she had to make sure that the one person who needed *her* was going to benefit.

The thought of telling Andreas about her sister, appealing to his humanity, was anathema. If anything, this evening had proved just how far Andreas was willing to go to seek his revenge. If she told him about Serena he might very well use her against Siena in some way, exactly as her father had. Siena shivered at the very thought. No way could she ever let that happen again.

She knew, though, that the very audacious plan forming in her head would ensure Andreas's hatred of her for ever.

Andreas's blood hummed with anticipation as he watched the woman who stood just feet away, her chin still lifted defiantly, even though they both knew she was about to give in.

She would be *his.* Her little act of pride had just been an exercise in proving to Andreas that he was still the last man she'd choose on earth, even if there was enough heat between them to melt an iceberg. And even if she *was* desperate.

His mouth tightened into a line. If anything it just proved that he was right: Siena wanted out of her challenging circumstances and back into the world she knew so well.

All *he* cared about was sating this burning desire inside him. Witnessing Siena DePiero swallow her pride and her denial of their mutual attraction would be a delicious revenge, and the very least he deserved after suffering so acutely at her hands.

'Well, Siena? What's it to be?'

Siena hated the smug tone of arrogance in Andreas's voice. She couldn't believe she was even contemplating what she was about to do, but assured herself she could do this. She had to.

In a way it should be easy—she'd merely be reverting to the type she'd played well for as long as she could remember: that of a privileged heiress with nothing more on her mind than the dress she'd wear to the next charity function. No one except for Serena had ever known of her deep hatred of that vacuous world where people routinely stabbed one another in the back to get ahead. Where emotions were so calcified that no reaction was genuine.

Before she could lose her nerve altogether, Siena blurted out, 'I will come with you—right now if you wish.' She saw Andreas's slow smile of triumph curling his mouth and said quickly, before he thought he was about to have everything his way, 'But I have terms for this…if we're to embark on…' Words failed her. She simply could not articulate what he wanted and expected. What she'd agreed to in her head.

He arched a dark brow. 'This affair? Becoming lovers? Companions?'

Siena flushed. The word *companions,* even though he'd

meant it sarcastically, struck her somewhere very deep and secret. They would never be companions.

Feeling agitated, she moved behind her one rickety chair, putting her hands on its back as if it could provide support. She nodded once, jerkily. 'Yes. I have terms.'

Andreas folded his arms across his chest. He looked almost amused, and Siena welcomed this as it made the fire grow in her belly. He only wanted her for one thing, and she was only exploiting him for his desire.

Baldly she declared, 'I want money.' And then she winced inwardly. She'd been brought up to be the ultimate society diplomat, yet here with this man she regressed to someone barely able to string a sentence together. She was too raw around him. She couldn't call up that fake polite veneer if her life depended on it.

As Andreas registered Siena's words something dark solidified in his gut. He should have expected this. A woman like Siena DePiero would never come for free. She would expect him to pay handsomely for the privilege of bedding her. As much as he'd paid for touching her in the first place.

Disgust evident in his voice, he said coolly, 'I've never paid for a woman in my life and I'm not about to start now.'

Siena went as pale as parchment and Andreas had to curb the urge to sneer. *How* could she look so vulnerable when she was effectively standing there asking for payment to be his mistress?

Two spots of colour bloomed then in her cheeks and bizarrely he felt comforted. He could see her struggling with whatever she wanted to say. Finally she got out, 'Those are my terms. I want a sum of money or else I'm not going anywhere—and if you come near me I'll scream the place down.'

His lip curled. 'Just like your neighbours? I didn't see anyone rush to *their* aid.'

Siena flushed more. It made Andreas bite out, 'Just how much money are we talking about?'

He saw Siena swallow and she licked her lips for a second, effortlessly drawing Andreas's eye to those lush pink swells and making that heat in his body intensify. Damn her, but he wanted her—possibly even at a price.

Siena felt sick. But she was too far gone to stop now. She saw the disgust etched in the lines of his starkly handsome face. He would despise her for this, but if he could despise her and still want her that was fine with her.

She named her price. The exact amount of money she would need to ensure Serena's care for a year. If she was going to do this then she had to make it worthwhile. Six months wouldn't be enough to ensure Serena's long-term recovery. A year in therapy and rehabilitation would.

Andreas whistled softly at the amount and Siena saw how his eyes became even icier. He came close again and she fought not to back away, her eyes glued to his. In a bizarre way, now that she'd said it, she found a weight lifting off her shoulders.

'You value yourself very highly.'

Siena burned. Shame came rushing back. Nevertheless, she tossed her head and said defiantly, 'What if I do?'

Andreas looked her up and down and walked around her. Siena could feel his eyes roving over her body.

He said from behind her, 'For that kind of money I think it would be within my rights to sample the goods again before making a decision, don't you? After all, that's just good business sense.'

Siena whirled around indignantly even as heat suffused every particle of her skin, but words got lodged in her throat. She would be the worst kind of hypocrite if she were to lambast him.

She could see that Andreas was livid, with dark colour slashing his cheeks. Before she could stop him he was snaking a hand around her neck and pulling her towards him. She had to go with it or fall off balance completely.

He ground out with disgust, 'I don't pay women for sex. I never have and I never will. It's heinous and disgusting and demoralising. Especially when you want it as much as I do...'

And with that his mouth was on hers and he was obliterating any sense of reality—again. Siena's thoughts were lost in a blaze of heat. Her hands were on Andreas's chest and he'd gathered her closer by curling his arm around her back, arching her into him, where she could feel the burgeoning evidence of his arousal against her belly.

His mouth was forcing hers open, and once that happened she didn't have a chance. His tongue found and tangled with hers, stroking along it, demanding a response. Siena mewled deep in her throat, almost pitifully. Andreas was possessing her with sensual mastery and, far from being disgusted, she found that her arms itched to climb higher, to curl around Andreas's neck, and her tongue was dancing just as hotly as his.

His hand left her waist and travelled up along her ribs. Siena was aware of an intense spiking of anticipation in her blood as her breasts seemed to swell in response, nipples peaking painfully, waiting for his touch.

But Andreas didn't cup her breast as she was suddenly longing for him to do. He stopped just short and pulled his head back. She opened her eyes with an effort, to see his, hot and molten, searing her alive, damning her for her audacity and stubborn denial of their attraction. Her breath was coming in rapid bursts and a million and one things were vying for supremacy in her brain, all of them urging her to pull away—fast. But she couldn't move.

Roughly he said, with disgust lacing his voice again, 'Much as I hate to admit it, I think that perhaps you might just be worth paying an astronomical amount of money to bed.'

He was the one to pull away, leaving Siena feeling adrift and wobbly.

He ran a hand through his hair and looked at her, his mouth taut with condemnation. 'You've learnt your lessons well, De-Piero…in the beds of however many countless lovers you've entertained. Were they the ones to teach you that intoxicating mix of innocence and artless sensuality designed to inflame a man?'

Siena looked at Andreas, stunned at his words. He had no idea. He couldn't tell her gauche responses were all too *real*. And she vowed then that he never would know—however she had to do it.

She fought to find some veneer of composure and said, as cynically as she could, considering she was shaking inwardly like a leaf, 'What else did you expect? A disgraced virgin heiress? This is the twenty-first century—surely you know better than most that virgins are as mythical as the knight on a white horse you just spoke of?'

Andreas stalked away from her, tension emanating from his body in waves. In that moment he hated her, and he hated himself, because he knew he didn't have the strength to just walk away and leave her here. To show her nothing but disdain. If he did he knew she would torment him in dreams for ever. He'd spent five years haunted by her. He had to have her—had to have this closure once and for all. And he despised himself for his weakness.

He looked at Siena and to his chagrin all of his previous thoughts were blasted to smithereens and rendered to dust. Her hair was tousled from his hands, her cheeks were rosy and her lips full and pouting, pink from his kisses. Her chest still rose and fell with uneven breaths and those glorious blue eyes flashed defiantly.

Andreas had the very strong urge to take her right here in this scummy flat—to turn that expression of defiance into something much more acquiescent. And he would if he thought that once would be enough. But he knew with a preternatural prickling of awareness that it wouldn't be enough. He hardened his resolve. She would *not* reduce him to such baseness.

Siena was slowly regaining control of herself. His words rang in her head: *'I don't pay women for sex. I never have and I never will. It's heinous and disgusting and demoralizing.'* The pity of it was she agreed with every word he'd said, and had to admit to respecting him for it.

She finally dragged her almost stupefied gaze from his and walked on very shaky legs back to the door, about to open it—because surely he would be leaving now, for good? Once again Siena didn't like the hollow feeling that thought brought with it.

Before she could open the door, Andreas said ominously, 'What do you think you're doing?'

Siena looked at him, the breath catching in her throat for a moment. 'But you just said you wouldn't pay…'

Andreas's face was like stone, his eyes so dark they looked navy. 'Yes, I did, and I meant it.'

Siena struggled to understand. 'So, what…?'

Andreas crossed his arms. 'There are other means of payment that aren't so…' his lip curled '…obvious.'

Something very betraying kicked in Siena's gut at the thought that he wasn't leaving her. 'What do you mean?'

'Gifts…' He smiled cynically. 'After all, how many women and men have benefited from the largesse of their lovers for aeons? You can do what you like with them when our relationship is over, and if that means converting them into the money you want so badly then you're welcome to do it.'

Suspicious now, and feeling supremely naive because she'd never been in this situation before, she said, 'Gifts…what kind of gifts?'

Andreas's jaw tightened. 'The expensive kind. Jewels. Like the ones you were wearing that night.'

Siena flushed to recall the priceless diamond earrings and necklace her father had presented her with on the evening of that exclusive debutante ball in Paris. They'd belonged to her mother, but had been seized by the authorities along with everything else she had owned.

Siena found herself feeling almost a sense of sick relief that he wouldn't just be handing her a sum of money. The thought of receiving jewellery made what she'd just asked for a little more palatable, despite the fresh shame heaped on top of old shame. Siena comforted herself with the thought that Andreas must have presented plenty of his lovers with tokens of his affection.

'Fine,' she said shakily, barely believing she was agreeing to this. 'I'll accept gifts in lieu of payment.'

Andreas smiled. 'Of course you will.'

Siena had a vision of walking out of here with him and fresh panic galvanised her to ask, a little belatedly, 'What.. what will you expect of me?' She held her breath.

Andreas's smile faded. He suddenly looked harsh, forbidding. Not like a man who wanted her in his bed so badly that he'd sought her out and was prepared to pay her in kind for it.

'Considering the price you've put on yourself…I will expect you to be a very willing, affectionate and inventive lover. I'm a very sexual man, Siena, and I pride myself on satisfying my lovers, so I expect the same in return. Especially from you.'

Siena struggled to hold down a hysterical giggle. *Inventive lover?* He'd be lucky if she managed not to betray her innocence, and she could imagine now with a lancing feeling of pain just how unwelcome *that* knowledge would be. It might even be enough to turn him off altogether. As tempted as Siena was to suddenly blurt out that intimate truth, she thought of her sister and clamped her mouth shut. No going back. Only forward to accept the consequences of her actions, which she'd set in motion five years before.

Not wanting to think of how his assertion that he was 'a very sexual man' had impacted her deep inside, Siena asked rather shakily, 'How long will you want me for?'

Andreas came close to Siena, where she stood near the door, and touched her jaw with his finger, making her shiver with helpless sensation. His eyes travelled up and down her body with dark intent and then rose back to hers.

With almost insulting insouciance he said, 'I think about a week should satisfy my desire for retribution and for you.'

Siena flinched minutely. There was a wealth of insult in his assumption that a week would be enough, and Siena hated that it felt like an insult when it should feel like a reprieve. Anyone could handle anything for a week. Even this.

'A week, then.' Siena assured herself that seven days was a blip in the ocean of her life. She could do it.

Andreas smiled, but it didn't reach those dark eyes. 'I'm already looking forward to this time next week, when the past truly will be in the past. For ever.'

Siena's sense of vulnerability increased. 'The feeling is mutual, believe me.'

After a tense moment Andreas dropped his hand, stepped back and said, 'Get your stuff packed, Siena, and don't leave anything behind.'

'But I'll be coming back here…'

Andreas's mouth thinned as he took in the meagre furnishings with a disdainful glance. 'You won't be returning here. *Ever.*'

Siena opened her mouth to protest and then stopped. Of course he thought she wouldn't be coming back here if she was going to turn his gifts into cash. Andreas didn't know that in a week's time she'd be as broke as she currently was, and she didn't want his razor-sharp brain to pick that up.

Faintly she assured herself that she'd worry about it when the time came and went into the tiny bedroom and pulled out her case. Only a few hours ago she'd had nothing more on her mind than how to get through the evening without keeling over from exhaustion and the constant niggling worry about how she would be able to look after Serena, because they didn't have enough money to continue paying for her psychiatric care.

But now her life had been turned upside down and she had a very unexpected and unwitting benefactor for Serena.

The next week stretched ahead like a term of penal servitude. But, treacherously, Siena felt a shiver of anticipation run through her. Would Andreas expect her to sleep with him tonight? The thought made her heart leap into her throat and her mouth went dry. She wasn't ready—not in a million years.

The thought of all that intense masculinity focused on her was overwhelming when she was so inexperienced. Siena felt numb as she started to pull the paltry collection of clothes from the rail. She didn't even have a wardrobe. She could almost laugh when she thought of the palatial bedroom she'd had all her life, with its medieval four-poster bed. It would have encompassed this entire flat about twice over…

A huge shadow darkened her bedroom door and Andreas rapped out with clear impatience, 'Actually, you can leave everything here. Unless there's something of sentimental value. I'll be supplying you with a new wardrobe.'

Siena just looked at Andreas. She saw an austerely handsome man, eager to get out of this hole of a place and take her with him so that he could mould her into what he wanted. He was so sure of himself now—a Titan of industry, used to having what he wanted when he wanted.

Siena didn't doubt that most of the women in Andreas's life were only too happy to comply with his demands, and she had to quash the dart of something dark at the thought of those women. Dismay gripped her. It wasn't jealousy. It couldn't be jealousy. She hated this man for what he was doing and what he'd become—he was welcome to his hordes of satisfied lovers.

Self-derision that she could allow this to happen to her and the knowledge that she had no choice because this was her only hope to help Serena made Siena's spine straighten. Tersely she bit out, 'Give me five minutes.'

CHAPTER FOUR

'WHAT WILL HAPPEN to my flat?'

Siena was trying not to notice Andreas's big hands on the steering wheel of his car, the way he handled it with such lazy confidence. Of course his car hadn't been on blocks when they'd gone outside. The young kid had been watching it like a hawk and had stared at Andreas as if he was a god.

Siena didn't know how to drive. Her father hadn't deemed it necessary. Why would she need to drive if she was going to be chauffeur-driven everywhere?

Sounding crisp, Andreas replied, 'I'll have my assistant settle up with your landlord. She can also inform your employers that you won't be coming back.'

Siena's hands tightened in her lap. In a way it was karma. She'd lost him his job and now he was losing her hers. Just like that. With a mere click of his fingers, Andreas was changing her life and ripping her very new independence out from under her feet. If she only had herself to worry about she wouldn't be here now, she assured herself inwardly, and hated the tiny seed of doubt that even then she could have held out against Andreas's will, or the guilt she felt.

She wondered what Andreas would have done if he'd known that she couldn't care less for his fortune? That his money wasn't for her at all? But she was forgetting that this man didn't care. Just as the younger man from five years ago hadn't cared. He'd only wanted her because it had been a coup to seduce one of the untouchable debutantes; their supposed virtue had been more prized and guarded than a priceless heirloom in a museum.

Except that virtue had been a myth. Siena had known all too well just how *touchable* the vast majority of her fellow debs had been. They'd looked innocent and pure, but had been anything but. She could recall with vivid clarity, how one of the girls—a princess from a small but insanely wealthy European principality—had boasted about seducing the porter who had brought her bags up to her room while her mother had slept in a drug-fuelled haze in the next room. She'd threatened the man with losing his job if he told anyone.

Siena's mouth hadn't dropped open—but only because her own sister had told her far more hair-raising stories than that, and had inevitably been a main participant when she'd been a debutante.

That evening she'd managed to escape from her father and had tried to find Andreas, to explain why she'd lied, hating herself for the awful falsehood. She'd explored an area reserved for staff only, and had come to an abrupt halt outside a half-open door when she'd heard a newly familiar voice saying heatedly, 'If I'd known how poisonous she was I'd never have touched her.'

A voice had pointed out coldly, 'You've done it now, Xenakis. You shouldn't have touched her in any case. Do you really think you would ever have had a chance with someone like her? She'll be married within a couple of years to one of those pale-faced pretty boys in that ballroom, or to some old relic of medieval Italian royalty.'

Andreas had said bitterly, 'I only kissed her because she was looking at me as if I was her last supper—'

The other voice came again, harder now. 'Don't be such a fool Xenakis. She seduced you because like every other spoilt brat in there she was bored—and you were game. Do you se-riously think she hasn't already got a string of lovers to her name? Those girls are not the innocents they seem. They're hardened and experienced.'

Siena had barely been breathing by then, her back all but flattened to the wall by the door. She'd heard Andreas emit an expletive and then she'd heard footsteps and fled, unable to countenance offering up an apology after that character assas-sination—after hearing his words, *'I only kissed her because she was looking at me as if I was her last supper.'*

The following morning Siena had woken early and felt stifled in her opulent bedroom. She'd dressed in jeans and a loose sweatshirt and had sneaked out through the lobby at dawn, with a baseball cap on her head in case she saw anyone she knew. She'd craved air and space—time to think about what had happened.

That searing conversation she'd overheard had been rever-berating in her head and she had run smack into a stone wall. Except it hadn't been a wall. It had been Andreas, standing beside a motorbike, in the act of putting on a helmet. Siena's baseball cap had fallen off, and she'd felt her long hair tumble around her shoulders, but shock had kept her rigid. In the cold light of day, in a black leather jacket and jeans, he'd looked dark and menacing. But she'd been captivated by his black eye and swollen jaw.

Startled recognition had turned to blistering anger. 'Don't look so shocked, sweetheart. Don't you recognise the work of your father's men? Don't you know they did this to avenge your honour?'

Siena had felt nauseous, and had realised why his voice had sounded so thick the previous evening. She should have known. Hadn't her father done the same thing, and worse, to her half-brother—his own son?

'I—' she'd started, but Andreas had cut her off with a slash of his hand through the air.

'I don't want to hear it. As much as I hate you right now, I hate myself more for being stupid enough to get caught. You know I've lost my job? I'll be lucky to get work cleaning toilets in a camping site after this…'

He'd burnt her up and down with a scathing look.

'I'd love to say that what we shared was worth it, but the only thing that would have made it remotely worth it is if you'd stopped acting the innocent and let me take you up against the wall of that dressing room as I wanted to. *Then* your father might not have caught us in the act.'

The crudeness of his words—the very confirmation that all the time she'd been quivering and shivering with burgeoning need, half scared to death, he'd assumed she was putting on some sort of an act and had wanted to take her standing up against the wall—had frozen Siena inside. Not to mention the excoriating knowledge that he'd merely made the most of an opportunity, and she'd all but thrown herself at him like some kind of sex-crazed groupie.

He'd taken her chin in his fingers, holding her tight enough to hurt, and he'd said, 'As the French say, *au revoir,* Siena De-Piero. Because some day our paths will cross again. You can be sure of that.'

He'd let her go, looked at her and uttered an expletive. With that he'd put on his helmet, swung his leg over the powerful bike and with a roar of the throttle had left her standing there, staring after him as if she'd been turned to stone.

The streets of London at night made Siena's memories fade. But the tangible anger she'd felt from Andreas that day would never fade.

'We're here.'

Siena looked to see that they were indeed pulling up outside

Andreas's apartment. Butterflies erupted in her belly. It felt as if aeons had passed since she'd been there already that evening.

The same young man who had parked the car earlier appeared to open her door. Siena was relieved, not wanting to touch Andreas. He was waiting as she emerged from the car with her one case in his hand. She couldn't stop him putting a hand to her back as he guided her into the apartment block. Futile anger burned down low inside her at being so vulnerable to this man…

Andreas was very aware of Siena's pale and tightly drawn features as they stood in the lift. He held her pathetically small case in his hand and had to quash the dart of something that felt ridiculously like pity at the knowledge that this was all she possessed now, when she had been one of the most privileged women in Europe. He reminded himself that this woman was one of the most invulnerable on the planet. She'd contrived every single moment of that evening in Paris, and when it had come to it she'd saved her own pretty neck.

Back in that grotty flat, when she'd asked how long this would last, Andreas had been about to say a month until he'd stopped himself. He'd never spent longer than a week with a lover, finding that he invariably needed his space or grew bored. So to find himself automatically assuming he'd need a *month* was unprecedented. He wanted Siena with a hunger that bordered uncomfortably on the obsessional, but there was no way she was going to turn out to be any different from his other lovers.

But, a snide inner voice pointed out, this was already different, because he was bringing her back to his apartment without even thinking about it. He'd never lived with a lover before. He'd always instinctively avoided that cloying intimacy. It made him feel claustrophobic. Andreas cursed himself now and wondered why he hadn't automatically decided to put Siena in a suite in a hotel, rather than bring her to his place. He didn't want to investigate his adverse gut reaction to that idea, when it was exactly what he *should* be doing.

Andreas hated that she was already making him question his motives and impulses. It made him think of dark, tragic memories and feelings of suffocation.

Before Andreas had left his home town at the age of seventeen he'd had a best friend who had been planning on leaving with Andreas. They were going to make something of themselves—*make a difference*. But that final summer his friend had fallen for a local girl and had become a slave to his emotions, telling Andreas he no longer wanted to travel or achieve anything special. He just wanted to settle down. Andreas had been incapable of changing his mind, and he'd watched his smart, ambitious friend throw away his hopes and dreams.

When his friend had found his girlfriend in bed with someone else he'd been so distraught that he'd killed himself. Andreas had been deeply affected by this awful violence. By the way someone could lose themselves so completely and invest so much in another person. *For love.* When that love hadn't even been reciprocated.

Andreas's own father had achieved a scholarship to a university in Athens—the first in his family to do so. But before he could go he'd met and fallen in love with Andreas's mother. She'd become pregnant and his father had decided to stay and get married, giving up his chance to study medicine.

Andreas had always been aware of his father's missed chance at another life. And after witnessing his friend's descent into horrific tragedy he'd been more determined than ever to leave. He had vowed never to let himself be sidetracked by *feelings*.

And he hadn't... Until he'd had far too close a brush with disaster in Paris, when he'd lost himself for a moment with a blonde seductress who had blown hot and then colder than the Arctic. She'd been a necessary wake-up call. A startling reminder of what was important. Not to get side-tracked.

Andreas reassured himself that this time things were different. When the lift stopped and the doors opened a rush of anticipaton and pleasure seized him, washing aside all his doubts. Siena DePiero was here and that was all he needed to know. Having her anywhere but close to him was not an option.

He'd been waiting for this moment for a long time—ever since that night, when he'd felt a kind of helpless anger and a sense of betrayal that he never wanted to feel again. Ever since that following morning, when she'd emerged from the hotel like a manifestation of his fantasies, her hair tumbled around her shoulders, backlit against the Paris dawn light. He'd wanted her then—fiercely. Even after what she'd done. It had taken all of his strength to get on his motorcycle and leave her behind.

'This is your room.'

Andreas was standing back to let Siena go into a vast bedroom. She'd just been given a tour of the jaw-dropping apartment. Silently she went in, relieved to hear Andreas say: *'your room'*. It was stunning, decked out in sumptuous but understated dark blues and complementary greys. A king-sized bed dominated the room, and Siena could see a glimpse of a white-tiled *en suite* bathroom and an entrance to another room.

Exploring, she found herself walking through a large dressing alcove to a separate lounge area, with a sofa, chairs, desk and a TV. Effectively she had her own suite.

She turned around to see Andreas leaning with his shoulder against the entrance to the dressing room, his hands in his pockets giving him a rakish air.

'This is…lovely,' she said stiffly, knowing that *lovely* was woefully inadequate in the face of this opulence. She was stunned again at Andreas's world now, and stunned anew to see him in his open-shirted tuxedo and realise that only hours before Andreas Xenakis had still been firmly in her shameful guilt-ridden past, not her tumultuous present.

But he was going to find you sooner or later, an inner voice reminded her.

'I'll arrange for a stylist and a beautician to come tomorrow, to attend to whatever you need.'

To make her beautiful for *him*.

Siena felt light-headed all of a sudden and swayed ever so slightly.

Immediately Andreas was standing straight, alert. 'What is it? Are you hungry?'

Siena beat back the waves of weakness, determined not to show Andreas any vulnerability. She shook her head. 'No. It's nothing. I'm just tired. I'd like to go to bed now.'

Andreas just looked at her for a long moment and then as if deciding something, he stepped back and said, 'By all means, Siena. You're my guest now and you know where everything is. Help yourself to anything you want.'

He backed away, and just before he got to her bedroom door he said softly, 'You should sleep while you can, Siena. You'll need it.'

Siena fought back a fresh wave of light-headedness at hearing him say that and watched as he walked out of the room, closing the bedroom door behind him. Sudden weariness nearly felled her. Her head hurt after everything that had happened. She couldn't take any more in.

Finding her small suitcase, she extracted what she needed and dressed for bed. She couldn't block out the way her weak body rejoiced to sink into expensive bedclothes, and gratefully slipped into what felt like a coma.

Andreas knew he was in the grip of a dream but he couldn't seem to pull himself out of it. He was back in that glittering ballroom in Paris. He could feel the ambition rising up within him to *own* such a place one day. It would be a remarkable achievement for a boy from a small town outside Athens with only the most basic qualifications to his name.

And then, like a camera zooming in for a close-up, all he could see was *her* face. Pure and beautiful. Haughty and cold. Perfect. The white-gold of her hair was in a complicated chignon. Jewels sparkled brilliantly at her neck and ears. Her profile was as regal as any queen. The only thing marring the picture was the blood-red stain of wine that was blooming outwards from her chest and up over her cleavage.

The dream faded and shifted, and now they were in that boutique, surrounded by mannequins in beautiful dresses and sparkling jewels behind locked displays. She was laughing, girlishly and innocently, huge blue eyes sparkling with mischief as she pointed to one of the mannequins and said imperiously, 'I want *that* one!'

Andreas bowed down in a parody of a manservant and she laughed even more, watching as he clambered into the window display to tussle with the mannequin and take off the dress. She was in fits of giggles now, watching him wrestle the stunning dress off the dummy before finally handing it to her with a flourish of triumph.

She curtseyed and said, with a flicker of those black lashes, 'Why, thank you, kind sir.' And then she vanished into the dressing room, pulling velvet folds of material behind her.

There was a fizzing sensation in his blood. Andreas felt buoyant when only minutes ago, surveying the crowd in the ballroom, he'd felt cynical...

And then she was there, in front of him again, and Andreas was falling into eyes so blue it hurt to look at them. And then the hurt became a real pain, and he looked down stupidly, to see a knife sticking out of his belly and blood everywhere.

He looked up and she was smiling cruelly. 'No, I did not ask you to touch me. I would never let someone like you touch me.'

His friend who had died, Spiro, was behind Siena, laughing at him. 'You thought you could remain immune?'

And then Andreas was falling down and down and down...

Andreas woke with a start, clammy with sweat, his heart pounding. He looked down and put a hand to his belly, fully anticipating seeing a knife and blood. But of course there was none. It was a dream. A nightmare.

He'd had that dream for months after he'd left France but not for a long time. He remembered. *Siena.* She was here, in his apartment. His heart speeded up again and he got out of bed, pulling on a pair of boxers. He assured himself that it was just her presence that had precipitated the dream again.

But it had left its cold hand across the back of his neck. He went into the darkened drawing room and poured himself some whisky, downing it in one. He slowly felt himself come back to centre, but was unable to shake the memory of that evening.

Andreas had been duty manager, overseeing the exclusive annual debutante ball, making sure it went without a hitch. He'd viewed all those beautiful spoilt young women with a very jaundiced eye, having heard all sorts of stories about their debauched ways.

Still, he'd barely believed them. They'd all looked so *innocent.* And none more so than the most beautiful of them all: Siena DePiero. He'd noticed that she was always slightly apart from the others, as if not part of their club. And the way her father kept her close at all times. He'd read her aloofness as haughtiness. And then he'd seen the moment when her dinner partner had accidentally spilled red wine all over her pristine white dress. Andreas had clicked into damage limitation mode and smoothly offered to take her to the boutique for a fresh dress.

Her father had been clearly reluctant to let her out of his sight but had had no choice. He wouldn't let his daughter be presented at the ball in a stained gown. And so Andreas had found himself escorting the cool beauty to the boutique, and had been very surprised when she'd confided huskily, 'Please excuse my father's rudeness. He hates any sort of adverse attention.'

Andreas had looked at her, taken aback by this politeness when he'd expected her to ignore him. Shock had cut through his cynicism because she'd looked nervous and blushed under his regard. To his complete embarrassment he'd found his body reacting to her…this very young woman, even though he'd known she wasn't that young. Her eighteenth birthday was the following day, and her father had already organised a brunch party with some of the other debutantes to celebrate.

He'd said something to put her at ease and she'd smiled. He'd almost tripped over his feet. By the time they'd reached the boutique his body had been an inferno of need. Siena had been chattering—albeit hesitantly and charmingly.

In the empty shop the sexual tension between them had mounted, instantaneous and strong enough to make Andreas reel. He'd had lovers by then—quite a few—and thought he knew women. But he'd never felt like that before. As if a thunderbolt had connected directly with his insides.

Her artless sensuality and apparent shyness had been at such odds with her cool and haughty beauty. With the reputation that had preceded her. That preceded all the debs every year.

She'd grimaced after a few minutes and looked around the shop, before glancing at a dress on a mannequin in the window. It was fussy-looking, but not far removed from what she wore.

'That's the one my father will approve of.'

She'd sounded so resigned and disappointed that Andreas had inexplicably wanted to see her smile again. He'd hammed it up, extricating the dummy from the dress. And he'd made her laugh.

Then she'd disappeared into the dressing room and Andreas had found every muscle in his body locked tight as he thought of her in a state of undress, fantasising about hauling back the curtain, pulling down his trousers, wrapping her legs around his hips and taking her there and then, against the wall…

And then she'd emerged and his blood had left his brain completely. She'd turned around and showed him a bare back, asking with a shy look over her shoulder, 'Can you do me up?'

To this day Andreas wasn't sure how he'd done it without pulling that dress down and off completely. But he hadn't. She'd turned round and some of her hair had been coming loose. He'd reached out and tucked one golden strand behind her ear and she'd blurted out, 'What's your name?'

Andreas had looked at her and said, 'Andreas Xenakis.'

She'd repeated his name and it had sounded impossibly sexy with her slight Italian accent. 'Andreas.'

And then all Andreas could remember was *heat* and *need*. His mouth had been on hers and she'd been clinging to him, moaning softly, sighing into his mouth, her tongue making a shy foray against his, making him so hard…

Andreas's mind snapped back to the present. He was holding his glass so tightly in his hand he had to relax for fear of shattering it. He grimaced at his body's rampant response just at the memory of what had happened and willed himself to cool down.

He looked out at the millionaire's view of London he could afford now. A far cry from his roots and from painful memories of lives wasted. His mouth twisted. *Wasted because of love.* But, strangely, his usual sense of satisfaction deserted him. Because a new desire for satisfaction had superseded it. For a satisfaction that would only come from taking Siena into his bed and sating himself with her.

He'd never forgotten the way she'd changed in an instant that night—from a she-witch, writhing underneath him, begging him to touch her and kiss her all over, to pushing him off as if his touch burnt her. The way she'd sprung up, holding her dress against her, looking at him accusingly. He'd only realised then that there was someone else in the room. Her father. Looking at him with those cold eyes, as if he were a piece of scum.

The dream and the memory made Andreas shiver. Because it reminded him of how duped he'd been that night. How, despite his better instincts, he'd let himself believe that Siena had really been that giggling, shy, artlessly sexy girl. And, worst of all, how she'd made him want to believe that girl existed.

He should have known better. He of all people. As soon as he'd started working in the city of Athens his looks had attracted a certain kind of sexually mature and confident woman. Inevitably wealthy. They'd offered him money, or promotion, and had laughed at his proud refusal to get help via their beds. One had mocked him. 'Oh, Andreas, one day that hubris will get you into trouble. You'll fall for a pretty girl who pretends not to be as cold and hard as the rest of us.'

And he had. He'd fallen hard. In front of Siena and her father that night. In all honesty Andreas hadn't truly become so cynical yet that he'd believed someone as young as Siena could be so malicious and calculating. But he'd watched her transform from shy sex kitten to a cold bitch. Colder than any of those other women he'd known. And just like that he'd grown his cynical outer skin and his heart had hardened in his chest.

Since then he'd surrounded himself with the kind of women who populated the world he now inhabited. The kind who were sexually experienced and worldly-wise. He had no time for women who played games or who pretended they were something they weren't. And he would never, *ever,* believe in the myth of sweet innocence again.

A flare of panic in his gut propelled Andreas out of the drawing room, setting down his glass as he did so. He went to Siena's bedroom door and opened it silently. It took a second for his eyes to adjust to the dimmer light, and when it did and he saw the shape on the bed his heart slowed. Relief made a mockery of all of his assurances that he was in control but he pushed it aside.

For a second he'd thought it part of the dream. That she wasn't really here. That he was still looking for her.

He found himself standing by her bed and looking down. She was on her back, hair spread out around her head, breathing softly, dressed only in a T-shirt. Her breasts were two firm swells that had the blood rushing to Andreas's groin *again*.

Triumph was heady. She was here. She would be his.

Andreas knew that if her father's business hadn't imploded the way it had he would have been equally determined to get to her, but it would have been much harder to get close.

In the dim light he could see dark shadows under her eyes and he frowned. She looked tired and he felt his chest constrict. Just then she moved slightly, making him tense. As she settled she snored softly. Andreas found his mouth tipping up at this most incongruous sound from one so perfect.

Then he remembered the way she'd asked for money and the smile faded. He had to remember who she was, how she had fooled him so easily into thinking she was something she was not. He'd already learnt his lesson and he wasn't about to repeat his mistake.

The following evening Siena was standing at the window of the main living area in Andreas's palatial apartment. She turned her back on the evocative dusky view of London's skyline and sighed. She couldn't be more removed from the hovel of a flat she'd been living in. But as much as she'd hated it, on some perverse level she'd loved it because it had been symbolic of her freedom.

And now once again she was incarcerated in a gilded prison. Andreas had already gone to work when she'd woken up that morning, and she'd been relieved not to have to deal with him when she still felt dizzy with how fast things had moved. He'd left a curt note, informing her that it was his housekeeper's day off but she must help herself to whatever she wanted, and that a stylist and a beautician would be arriving later that morning.

Sure enough, a couple of hours later two scarily efficient-looking women had arrived, and within hours Siena had been waxed, buffed and polished. She now had a dressing room full of clothes, ranging from casual right up to *haute couture.* Not to mention cosmetics, accessories and lingerie so delicate and decadent it made her blush. And shoes—a whole wall of shoes alone.

The sheer extravangance had stunned Siena. Her father had been extremely tight with his money, so while she and Serena had always been decked out in the most exclusive designs it had been to perpetuate an image—nothing more.

Andreas had called a short while before and informed her that there should be some beef in the fridge. He'd instructed her to put it in the oven so they could eat it when he returned to the apartment. Siena had just spent a fruitless half-hour trying to figure out which furturistic-looking steel appliance was the oven, to no avail.

She went back into the kitchen now, to try again, and started to go hot with embarrassment at her pathetic failing when she still couldn't figure it out. Her father had forbidden Siena and her sister ever to go near the kitchen of the *palazzo,* considering it a sign of a lack of class should either of his daughters ever know its ins and outs.

Before Siena had a chance to explore further she heard the

apartment door open and close and distinctive strong foot-falls. She tensed and knew Andreas had to be in the door-way, looking at her. She turned around slowly and fought to hide her reaction to seeing him in the flesh again, dressed in a dark suit. His sheer good looks and charisma reached out to grab her by the throat. She could feel her body respond-ing, as if it had been plugged into an energy source coming directly from him to her.

Siena retreated into attack to disguise her discomfiture. She lifted her chin and crossed her arms. 'I didn't put the beef in the oven because I refuse to be your housekeeper.'

Andreas regarded her from the doorway. Siena noticed that his jaw was darkly stubbled in the soft light. He was so in-tensely masculine and her blood jumped in response.

'Well, then,' he said with deceptive lightness as he came further into the room, his hair gleaming under the lights, 'I hope you had a decent lunch today. Because I refuse to be your chef just because you can't be bothered to take something out of the fridge and put it in the oven.'

At that moment Siena felt an absurd rush of self-pity. She was actually starving, because she'd only had a sandwich ear-lier, but she clamped her mouth shut because she knew she was acting abominably. And if she had no intention of telling him why then she had no one to blame but herself. She would spend all day tomorrow working out where the blasted oven was and how to work it even if it killed her.

Lying through her teeth, and trying desperately not to look at the succulent lump of meat he was taking out of the fridge, Siena said loftily, 'I'm not hungry anyway. In fact I'm quite tired. It's been a long day. I'm going to go to my room, if you have no objections.'

Andreas looked up from his ministrations and said easily, 'Oh, I object all right. I think you could do with being forced to watch me eat after your pettish spoilt behaviour, but the expression on your face might put me off my food.'

He went on coolly. 'As it happens I have some work to continue here this evening...so feel free to entertain yourself. You don't have to confine yourself to your room Siena, like some kind of martyr.'

She turned and walked out, not liking the way Andreas was dealing with preparing himself dinner so dextrously. It caused something to flutter deep inside her. She didn't like these little signs that Andreas couldn't be boxed away so neatly.

She was about to go towards her room when she found herself seeking out the more informal sitting area that Andreas had shown her the previous evening. She forced herself to relax in front of the TV, even though she really wanted to escape to her room and avoid any more contact with Andreas.

A short time later Andreas gave up any attempt to work. It was impossible when he knew that Siena was somewhere nearby. He shook his head again at her spoilt behaviour. He didn't know why it had surprised him, but it *had*. It was as if some stubborn part of him was still clinging onto the false image of that sweet girl in Paris, before she'd morphed into the spoilt heiress.

He got up and put his cleared dinner plate in the dishwasher in the kitchen, noticing as he did that nothing else had been touched. His mouth flattened into a hard line at this further evidence of Siena's stubbornness. She was too proud for her own good. He walked back out and stopped when he heard the faint sound of canned laughter. He followed the sound and found Siena curled up on the couch, fast asleep. Her lashes cast long dark shadows on her cheeks.

Absently Andreas found the remote and switched the TV show off. Siena stirred but didn't wake. He'd been blocking out how it had felt to see her in his kitchen when he'd come home earlier. Dressed in softly worn jeans and a T-shirt. Hair in a ponytail. Bare feet. He wasn't sure what he'd expected but it hadn't been that. He wasn't used to women dressing down, but told himself that she was obviously making a petty point, refusing to make an effort for him.

He knew Siena had seen the beautician, and inevitably his mind wandered to the parts of her body that would be sleek, smooth. He hadn't noticed any discernible physical difference but then, he reminded himself cynically, it was hard to improve on perfection. And even as she was now, asleep on a couch in jeans and a T-shirt, she *was* perfection.

Andreas saw her hands now and bent down. They looked softer already, and he could see that her bitten nails had been cleaned up, but they had been filed very short. He felt that constriction in his chest again at noticing that.

And then suddenly she was awake, looking up at him with those huge startling blue eyes. For a moment something crackled between them, alive and powerful. And then he saw Siena register where she was and with whom. The way she grew tense and her eyes became wary. He straightened up.

Siena struggled to a sitting position, more than discomfited to find Andreas watching her so coolly while she slept. 'What time is it?' Her voice felt scratchy.

He flicked a glance at his watch. 'After midnight.'

Siena stood up and only realised then how close she was to Andreas, and how tall he was when she was in bare feet. 'I should go to bed.'

'Yes,' he observed. 'You seem to be extremely tired. It must have been all that pampering and choosing dresses today.'

Siena was about to protest at the unfairness of his attack, and inform him of just how hard she had been working, but the words died in her throat. He was too close all of a sudden, those dark navy eyes looking at her and reminding her of another time when they'd stood so close and she'd breathed, *'Andreas...'*

She moved back suddenly, but forgot about the couch behind her and felt herself falling back. With the reflexes of a panther Andreas reached out and circled her waist with his hands, hauling her against him.

The breath whooshed out of Siena's mouth. Her hands were on his chest and he felt hot to the touch even through his shirt. 'What...' Her mouth went dry at the thought that he might kiss her. 'What are you doing?'

'What I'm doing, Siena, is...' He stopped and the moment stretched between them.

Siena fancied she could hear both their hearts beating in unison. In that moment she wanted him with a sudden fierce longing deep in her abdomen. She was mesmerised by his mouth. She wanted him to kiss her. And that knowledge burned inside her...

'...letting you go to bed.'

CHAPTER FIVE

ANDREAS HAD PUT Siena away from him before she'd realised what he was doing and instantly she felt foolish. She blushed and he raised a brow.

'That really is some skill—to be able to blush at will. But you forget that it's wasted on me, Siena. I'm a sure thing. You don't have to pretend with me.'

Siena's betraying flush increased—with anger now. 'That's good to know. I won't waste my energy, then.'

She whirled around to leave but was caught when Andreas reached out to take her hand. Electricity shot up her arm. She looked back warily.

'Actually, I have something for you. Come with me.'

Curious, Siena followed Andreas into his huge dimly lit study. It was a beautiful room, very masculine, with floor-to-ceiling shelves that heaved with books. He had the latest high-spec computers and printers.

He'd gone to a picture in the corner and pulled it out from the wall to reveal that it hid a safe. He entered the combination and pulled out a long velvet box. He came over and opened it, so that Siena could see that it was a stunningly simple yet obviously very expensive diamond bracelet.

Her heart thumped once, hard, and she felt a little sick. Andreas was taking it out and reaching for her wrist so that he could put it on. He said coolly, 'You've been here for one night already. I don't see why I can't reward you.'

Feeling very prickly, and not liking the way the cool platinum and stones sat against her pale wrist, winking brilliantly, Siena said acerbically, 'You don't have to reward me as if I'm a child, Andreas.'

He dropped her wrist and looked at her, his eyes turning dark. 'I know you're not a child, Siena. I'm rewarding you because you asked me to. Tomorrow evening we are going to a charity function in town...tonight will be the last night you sleep alone.'

Trepidation and fear were immediate. The thought of being seen and recognised, having people point and whisper about the disgraced DePieros... But Siena wouldn't let Andreas see how much it terrified her, or let him see how even more terrifying she found the thought that this time tomorrow night she would be in his bed...

Siena backed away. 'I can't wait.'

She'd almost got to the door when Andreas called her name again. She took a deep breath and turned around.

'I've arranged for one of London's top jewellers to come to the apartment tomorrow morning.' His jaw tightened. 'You can choose a selection of jewels to your hard little heart's content.'

Siena said nothing. She suddenly looked starkly pale and whirled around, walking quickly out of the room. Andreas watched her go and had to relax his hands because they'd clenched to fists. Once again he wasn't sure what kind of reaction he'd expected, but it hadn't been that.

He had to take a deep breath, and he wondered why he wasn't following his base instincts and taking her here and now. Either on the couch earlier, or here in his office. Or following her to her bedroom. She was here. She was his. She was making him pay for it. But he wouldn't do it now. Because she made him feel a little wild and out of control.

She reminded him far too easily of the raw, ambitious young man he'd once been. Desperate to be a part of the world she'd so easily inhabited because he'd believed that if he was, then he'd truly be as far away from stagnating in his home town as he could possibly be. But he'd changed since then. Being forced into exile had made him appreciate his home and where he came from. It had given him a more balanced view.

He might not want to be a part of his family's cosy, settled world, but he respected it and their choices. A tiny voice mocked him, reminding him that sometimes when he went back now he found himself feeling a pang when he saw the interaction between his sisters and their husbands and children. It even made him feel slightly threatened—as if, if he stayed too long, everything he'd worked for would disappear and he'd become that young man again, with nothing to his name.

He would not let Siena bring back those memories or reduce him to such baseness. She'd done it once before, before he'd even realised what was happening, and she'd torn his world apart.

No, he would be urbane and civilised—all the things he'd become since he'd stood before her in Paris and been made to feel utterly helpless, at the mercy of the huge emotions seething inside his gut. She didn't have that power over him any more and she never would.

Back in her room, Siena struggled to get the diamond bracelet off but refused to go and ask Andreas for help. She was far too volatile when in close proximity to him. Finally it sprang free and Siena put it down with a kind of fascinated horror. He'd given her a diamond bracelet—just like that. Tomorrow he'd be giving her a lot more. And tomorrow night…

Siena sank back down onto the end of the bed and crossed her arms over her belly.

She wanted to hate Andreas for this…but she had no real

reason to hate him. So he'd used her five years ago, when she'd all but thrown herself at him...? What young red-blooded man wouldn't have done the same? It wasn't his fault it had meant nothing to him. She was the one who had imbued the situation with a silly fantasy that something special had happened between them. Had he deserved to lose his job and be beaten up over it? *No.*

She shivered when she thought of that young beaten man, getting on his bike to ride away that dawn morning, and the man he'd become now. For a second that morning, despite his anger, Siena had had a fantasy of getting on the back of that bike with him and fleeing into the dawning light. If she hadn't had to think of her sister she might well have done it.

Siena knew very well that if Andreas hadn't stopped kissing her the other night in her flat he would have had her there and then, realised that she was woefully inexperienced, and most likely walked away without a backward glance, having satisfied his curiosity and his desire for revenge. Treacherously, that thought didn't fill her with the kind of relief it ought to.

What happened to her when he touched her was scary. It was as if he short-circuited her ability to think rationally. When she'd woken on the couch earlier and found him staring at her she'd reacted viscerally: her blood humming and her body coming alive. There hadn't been a moment's hesitation in that acceptance. And then she'd realised where she was and why and reality had come tumbling back...

Andreas's restraint towards her told her that he was in far more control of this situation than she was. The thought of going out in public...the thought of Andreas making love to her... Siena would have to call on that well-worn icy public persona—the one her father had so approved of because it made her seem untouchable and aloof. Desirable. Unattainable.

She clenched her hands to fists. The only problem was,

she was all too attainable. The minute Andreas touched her *aloof* and *icy* went out of the window to be replaced with heat and insanity.

Much to Siena's relief, when she woke and went exploring in the morning there was no sign of Andreas initially—but her skin prickled with that preternatural awareness that told her he was somewhere in the apartment. She figured he might be in his study, and made sure to avoid going near it.

To her added relief there was an array of breakfast things left out in the kitchen, but she didn't like the way her belly swooped at the thought that he'd done this for her. She poured herself some coffee, which was still hot, and took a croissant with some preserves over to the table and sat down.

'Nice of you to join the land of the living. I was beginning to think I might need a bucket of cold water to wake you.'

Siena looked up and nearly choked on her croissant. She hadn't even heard him coming in, and to see him dressed in jeans and a dark polo shirt moulded to his impressive chest was sending tendrils of sensation through every vein in her body.

She swallowed with difficulty, but before she could say anything Andreas was looking at his watch and saying, with not a little acerbity, 'Well, it *is* ten a.m., I expect this is relatively early for you?'

Siena fought down a wave of hurt as she thought of how hard she'd been working for the last few months. Usually by now she'd have done half a day's work. But of course he was referring to her previous life. In fact she'd always been an early riser, up before anyone else. What she wasn't used to, however, was the current exhaustion she was feeling, thanks to the unaccustomed hard work. And that made her angry at herself for being so weak.

She kept all of this hidden and said to Andreas sweetly,

'Well, I'd hate to disappoint you. Tomorrow I can make it midday, if you like?'

He prowled closer, after helping himself to more coffee, and said, 'I'd like it very much if we were in bed together till one o'clock.'

It took a monumental effort not to react to his provocative statement. He was so *audacious*. He sat down at the table, long legs stretched out, far too close to Siena's. She fought the urge to move her own legs.

'Yes, well, I can't imagine you neglecting your business to that level.' After all, she knew well how her father had consistently relegated his children to the periphery, only to be trotted out for social situations.

She looked away from that far too provocatively close rangy body and concentrated on eating the croissant.

'Don't worry,' Andreas commented drily, 'my business is doing just fine.'

Siena flashed back, 'At the expense of all those poor people who are losing their jobs just because of your insatiable ambition.'

Andreas's eyes narrowed on her and Siena cursed herself. Now she'd exposed herself as having followed his progress.

'So you read the papers? I would have thought that you should know better than to believe everything you read in print. And since when have you been concerned with the *poor people?*'

There was ice in his tone, but also something more ambiguous that sounded like injured pride, and Siena felt momentarily confused. A sliver of doubt pierced her. Weren't those stories true?

Andreas uncoiled his tall length, and stood up, going to the sink, where he washed out his cup—a small domestic gesture that surprised Siena.

He turned and said, 'The jeweller will be here shortly.'

He'd walked out before Siena could respond, and she watched his broad back and tall body disappear, radiating tension. She felt wrong-footed. As if she should apologise!

Siena took her things to the sink, where she washed up perfunctorily and thought churlishly that at least she could figure out the taps. Just as she was turning to leave an older lady walked in, smiling brightly. 'Morning, dear! You must be Ms DePiero. I'm Mrs Bright, the housekeeper.'

Siena smiled awkwardly and said, 'Please call me Siena…'

As accomplished as she was in social situations, Siena was an innately shy person and came forward faltering slightly. The older woman met her halfway and took her hand in a warm handshake, smiling broadly. Siena liked her immediately and smiled back.

Siena wisely took the opportunity to ask Mrs Bright about the kitchen, and liked the woman even more when her eyes rolled up to heaven and she said in a broad Scots accent, 'I thought I'd need a degree in rocket science to figure it all out, but it's actually very simple once you know.'

When Siena explained about the previous evening Mrs Bright said conspiratorially, 'Don't worry, pet. I couldn't work out which one was the oven either at first.'

Unbeknown to the two women, who were now bent down by the oven, Andreas had come back to the doorway. He listened for a moment and then said abruptly, 'The jeweller is here, Siena.'

The two women turned around and he could see the dull flush climbing up Siena's neck. He flashed back to the previous evening, when he'd found her looking so defiant in the kitchen, refusing to put the meat in the oven.

She said thank you to the housekeeper and walked over to him. Andreas caught her arm just as she was about to pass and said, *sotto voce,* 'You didn't know where the oven was. Why didn't you just tell me?'

He could see Siena's throat work, saw that flush climb higher, and felt curiously unsteady on his feet.

Eventually she bit out, avoiding his eye, 'I thought you'd find it funny.'

Andreas didn't find it funny in the least. He said, 'You could have told me, Siena. I'm not an ogre.'

Siena was trembling by the time they got to the drawing room, where Andreas had directed her. Two small men were waiting for them, with lots of cases and boxes around them and an array of jewels laid out on a table before them. Siena noticed a security guard in the corner of the room. She felt sick.

Later that evening Siena was waiting for Andreas. He'd gone to his office that morning after the jewellery show-and-tell, and she'd been left with a small ransom's worth of jewellery. A special safe had been installed in Andreas's office just for her use.

She still felt jittery. Andreas had insisted that to fully appreciate whether or not the jewellery was suitable Siena should get changed into an evening gown. He'd led her, protesting, into her dressing room and picked out a long black strapless dress.

'Put this on.'

Siena had hissed, 'I will not. Don't be so ridiculous. I'll know perfectly well what will suit me and what won't.'

'Well, seeing as I'm paying for the privilege of your company this week, I'd like to see you try out the jewellery in more suitable garb than jeans and a T-shirt—which, by the way, I expect to be in the bin by the end of today.'

'You're just doing this to humiliate me.' Siena had crossed her arms mulishly and glared at Andreas, who had looked back, supremely relaxed.

'Put the dress on, Siena, and put your hair up. Or I'll do it for you. I'll give you five minutes.'

With that chilling command he'd turned and walked out of

the room. Siena had fumed and resolved to do no such thing. But then an image of Andreas, striding back into her room and bodily divesting her of her jeans and T-shirt, had made her go hot. He wouldn't, she'd assured herself. But a small voice had sniggered in her head. *Of course he would.*

Gritting her teeth and repeating her mantra—*one week, one week*—Siena folded her jeans and T-shirt into her small suitcase, with no intention of following his autocratic command to throw them away, and slipped on the dress. It was simple in the way that only the best designer dresses could be, and beautifully made. Gathered under her bust in an Empire line, it flowed in soft silken and chiffon folds to the floor.

The bodice part of it clung to her breasts, making them seem fuller, and was cut in such a way as to enhance her cleavage. Siena had felt naked. Her father would never have allowed her to wear something so revealing…so sensual.

She'd pulled her hair back into a ponytail and returned to the salon barefoot. When the two jewellers had stood up on her return Siena had barely noticed, only aware of the dark blue, heavy-lidded gaze that had travelled down her body with a look so incendiary she'd almost stumbled.

Andreas had taken her hand and pulled her in beside him on a small two-seater couch, his muscular thigh far too close to hers through the flimsy covering of her dress. His arm had moved around her, his fingers grazing the bare skin of her shoulder, drawing small circles, making her breath quicken and awareness pierce her deep inside.

She'd cursed him and tried to move away—only to have him clamp his hand to her waist, pulling her even more firmly against him, so that her breasts had been crushed to his side and she'd been acutely aware of how hard his chest felt. The way his big hand curled possessively around her, fingers grazing her belly.

The jewellery itself had been a blur of glittering golds and diamonds, pearls, sapphires and emeralds. Andreas had picked things out and taken Siena's wrist to slip jewelled bracelets on, before adding them to a growing pile. When he'd put necklaces around her neck his hands had trailed softly across her bare shoulders, his fingers lightly touching her collarbone. Siena's face had flamed. It had felt like such an intimate touch.

She had tried to hold herself as rigidly as possible, aghast at how much it was affecting her to be subjected to what were relatively chaste touches. They'd been under the beady eyes of the jewellers, but Siena had had to remind herself they were being observed.

Losing count of the mounting pile of jewellery, Siena had been ready to scream by the time Andreas had tried a simple platinum and diamond necklace and matching bracelet on her and said, 'Wear this dress and these jewels tonight.'

She had bitten back a retort—a knee-jerk reaction to being dictated to. Her new-found sense of independence had surged forth, but then she'd reminded herself that he'd bought her. Therefore he could have her any which way he wanted. She'd had a very disturbing image of herself, naked, splayed across Andreas's bed, dressed in nothing but all these jewels.

When Andreas had finally declared himself satisfied the other men had started to gather up the remaining jewellery. But Siena had spotted something out of the corner of her eye. A flash of something delicate and golden. Before she could stop herself she'd reached out to touch the necklace, hidden in folds of velvet.

As she'd lifted it out it had become clear that it didn't have the same glittering *wow* factor of the other gems, but it was exquisite: a simple golden chain with a wrought-gold birdcage detail. The tiny filigree door was open and further up the chain was a bird flying, suspended. Siena's belly had clenched. Something about the bird flying out of its cage had resonated deeply within her.

The senior jeweller had cleared his throat uneasily. 'That's actually not meant to be part of the display we brought today. It was included by accident. It's by a Greek jeweler…'

'Angel Parnassus.' Siena had said, half absently. She knew the famous delicately crafted designs of the renowned jeweler and had always admired them.

'Yes…' the man had confirmed.

'We'll take that too,' Siena had heard Andreas say brusquely.

She'd started to protest, hating that Andreas had witnessed her momentary distraction and vulnerability. She'd looked at him and his eyes had been hard.

'It's a fraction of the price of the earrings you'll wear to-night. Have it if you like it so much, Siena.'

Siena hadn't wanted anything for *herself,* but she'd had no chance to speak. Andreas had already been standing up, shaking hands with the two men, seeing them out, leaving her with the necklace clutched in her hand.

Siena heard a noise now and tensed, her attention brought back to the present. Andreas had arrived a short while before, knocking on her door to check that she was nearly ready. When she'd swallowed the frog in her throat and assured him that she was, he'd disappeared—presumably to get ready himself. Siena was waiting in the drawing room, feeling ridiculously nervous at the thought of the evening ahead. This was a situation she'd never experienced before.

She was wearing the black dress, as decreed by Andreas. But when it had come to the jewels Siena had had a moment of rebellion. Instead of the diamond necklace and bracelet he'd wanted her to wear she'd picked out a bold diamond and sapphire necklace, with a matching cuff bracelet.

Somehow the brashness of the necklace felt like some kind of armour. But then Siena heard a familiar footfall behind her and any illusion of armour went out of the window.

* * *

When Siena turned to face Andreas he felt as if someone had just punched him in the belly. For a second he couldn't breathe. He'd dreamed of her so often like this…as he remembered her… Stunningly beautiful, elegantly aloof. Untouchable in a way that made him ache to touch her.

Her hair was drawn back and up into a high bun, effortlessly simple and yet the epitome of classic grace. Her make-up was understated, perfect. Nothing so brash as red lipstick. She didn't need it. The drama came from her cool blonde perfection.

His eyes narrowed on her necklace and a spurt of something hot went through him. 'You have defied me.'

Siena's chin hitched up minutely. 'You may have all but bought me for a week, but that does not mean I can't exercise some free will.'

Andreas inclined his head and tamped down on the hotness inside him. 'Indeed. That necklace is equally…beautiful.'

He had to admit that it set off her rather understated appearance with just the right amount of *élan*. The thick collar piece was studded with tiny diamonds and it curled around her neck and throat in a sinuous line down to where an enormous sapphire pendant hung against the creamy pale skin of her upper chest. The dark blue of the precious stone inevitably made the lighter blue of her eyes pop out.

Andreas pushed down the niggling vague doubts he'd had all day, ever since he'd overheard the conversation between her and Mrs Bright in the kitchen, when he'd learned that Siena had preferred to appear like a spoilt brat rather than reveal she didn't know where the oven was.

And then her reaction to the jewellery hadn't been the unmitigated greed and glee he'd expected to see. Siena had barely looked at the impressive array of jewellery, and the one thing that had caught her eye had been a simple gold pendant. Exquisite, yes, but not in the same league as the other jewels at all.

Andreas put such disturbing thoughts out of his head now. She hadn't shown much interest in the jewellery because she would be converting it all into cold hard cash within days. How could he forget that?

More importantly, by tonight all that cool, untouchable beauty would have come undone. She would be bucking against him and begging for release. She would no longer look so pristine. She would be as naked and sated as he intended to be. Flushed and marked by his passion.

His blood surged. He put out his hand. 'Come. It's time to go.'

A couple of hours later, after a sumptuous sit-down dinner, Siena was standing at Andreas's side and it felt as if her skin was slowly going on fire. Since he'd taken her hand in his in the apartment to lead her out he hadn't stopped touching her. Even if it was just a hand at the small of her back to guide her into the ultra-luxe Grand Wolfe Hotel, where the charity dinner banquet was taking place.

For someone who generally shied away from physical contact, because she'd never really experienced it growing up, Siena was dismayed at how much her body seemed to gravitate towards Andreas's touch. She wished pettily that she could break out in a rash, allergic to his touch.

'Drink?'

She looked at Andreas to see him holding out a glass of champagne. Siena shook her head. After a couple of glasses of wine with dinner, and an aperitif of Prosecco when they'd arrived, her head was feeling woozy enough. Andreas merely shrugged and put the glass back on a passing waiter's tray.

'Uncomfortable?'

Siena looked at Andreas again. For a second she thought

he meant in her dress or shoes, but then she saw the gleam in his eye and thought to herself, *Bastard*. She schooled her expression. 'I'm perfectly comfortable, thank you, considering the level of public interest in seeing who your new mistress is, and the realisation that she is one of the disgraced DePieros.'

Siena knew Andreas had to be aware of the way people had been looking and pointing all evening. The way a hush would fall when she came close, only to spark a flurry of whispers as they passed.

'Don't tell me it's actually *affecting* you? The debutante who so coldly excised a momentary mistake from her life?'

Andreas's voice was mocking and Siena held herself stiffly. She hadn't known just how much it would affect her to be in public again, exposed to people's excoriating judgement, but could she blame them? Even now as she caught someone's eye they looked away hurriedly.

Her voice was cool. 'Why would I deny you your moment of public retribution? No doubt this is highly entertaining for you.'

She turned and looked up into his face properly, making his hand which had been resting on the small of her back fall away. It was a tiny pathetic triumph.

'Perhaps,' she said, 'you should consider taking me to Rome to get the full effect of people's censure? After all, here in London I'm relatively unknown.'

Andreas's eyes flashed and he effortlessly put his arm around her and pulled her tight in against him, making Siena gasp softly. His body was so lean and hard. Like a wall of muscled steel. And against her belly she could feel the potent stirring of his body. Inside she went hot.

'I think it's time we danced.'

Before she could even remember what they'd been talking about Andreas was pulling Siena in his wake onto the dance floor, where other couples were already dancing in the seductively dim light. A very smooth jazz band were playing, but Siena hardly even registered the music as Andreas swung her round and into his arms, holding her close.

Siena tried to pull back in his embrace but it was impossible. His arm was a steel band high across her back and her hand was held high in his, against his chest. Dark blue eyes glittered down into hers and reminded her of the deep blue of the sapphire pendant that swung against her chest, the thought leaving a tart taste in her mouth. But even that couldn't impinge when she was this close to Andreas, breathing his evocative masculine scent deep.

Feeling his body harden even more against hers was rendering her completely defenceless. How could she remain immune to this level of sensual attack? This was his punishment, his revenge, right here on this dance floor. Making her mute with aching need and a burning desire which seemed to writhe within her like a coiled snake. Everything else fell away, and she was suddenly terrified that she wouldn't be able to contain this feeling. It was as if they were enclosed in a bubble, completely separate from everyone around them, even though Siena was dimly aware that Andreas was steering them expertly around the floor.

She'd danced with plenty of men since that debutante ball in Paris, usually propelled into their arms reluctantly by her father, but no dance had ever felt this raw or carnal. Andreas's hand on her back rested against bare skin and she could feel his fingers stroking rhythmically, making her legs weaken and the secret apex between them grow hot and wet.

This went far beyond what she'd felt that evening in Paris, when this same man had aroused her with just a look and a sexy smile. She'd been too young then to truly be able to handle everything he'd aroused within her. Now she knew he'd unleashed a completely alien part of her—a part of her that felt wild and needy, aching for something she'd never known before. She'd always found it so easy to be detached, contained, until she'd met him. And all that was rushing back now.

At that moment Andreas stopped, and Siena realised that the music had also stopped. The air crackled between them and Siena knew with a fatalistic feeling in her belly that this was it.

Eyes locked with hers, Andreas said huskily, 'It's time to go.'

Keeping her hand in his, Andreas swiftly negotiated their way off the dance floor. Siena felt as if she couldn't really breathe. Her skin prickled and felt hot. Her belly was tight. Somehow, magically, someone appeared to hand Siena her wrap, and she took it with both hands, pathetically grateful that Andreas wasn't touching her for just a second.

But then her hand was in his again and he was leading her out into the cool spring air. His car was already waiting by the kerb, its back door held open by a hotel doorman.

Once they were in the car it pulled away smoothly from the glittering hotel.

Andreas said curtly to his driver, 'Tom, some privacy, please.'

Instantly Siena saw the silent glide of the black partition cutting them off from the driver. She looked at Andreas and his eyes glowed in the dim light. He looked feral, wild, and her heart beat wildly in her chest.

'Come here,' he instructed throatily.

CHAPTER SIX

PANIC GRIPPED SIENA. She wasn't ready for this. Threadily she answered, 'No.'

Andreas arched a brow. His voice was deceptively mild. 'No?'

Siena shook her head, and then words were tumbling out. 'Look, you can't just expect that I'm going to—'

But her words were stopped mid-flow when Andreas reached across almost lazily and took her by the waist. He slid her along the seat until their thighs were touching. His hands felt huge around her and her eyes were locked with his. The air around them felt heavy and dense, thick with something Siena didn't really understand.

But when Andreas raised his hands up her body, brushing against the curves of her breasts, and slanted his mouth across hers Siena understood what it was. It was desire, and suddenly she was alive with it. Humming all over. It thickened her blood, forcing it through veins and arteries, pooling low in her pelvis, between her legs.

Her hands had been up, almost in a gesture of self-defence, but now Siena found herself putting them on Andreas's chest, to balance herself when he tugged her forward so that she half lay across him. She couldn't concentrate, couldn't think beyond the hot slide of his mouth against hers, and her mouth opened of its own volition under his.

Their tongues touched and Siena's hands curled into his shirt, bunching it unconsciously, seeking something to hold onto when she felt as if she were falling down and down.

One of Andreas's hands went down to her back and pulled her into him, making her arch against him. She was dimly aware that his other hand had moved up, was undoing her hair so that it fell around her shoulders, sensitising nerve-ends that were already tingling.

The kiss grew hotter. Andreas's tongue stabbed deep. His hand was tangled in her hair now, and he pulled back gently so that he could claim even more access. Siena couldn't hear anything through the blood roaring in her head and ears. When Andreas's mouth left hers she heard a low moan and only seconds later realized it was coming from her.

By then his mouth was trailing hot kisses across her jaw and he was pulling her head back even more, to press his mouth against her throat and down to where she could feel her pulse beat against his tongue.

Siena had the barest sensation of her dress feeling looser before she realised that Andreas had pulled the zip down at the back. He lifted his head and leant back for a moment. Siena tried to force some air into her lungs, but they seized again when she felt him pull down the bodice of her dress to reveal one naked breast.

They were in a cocoon. Siena wasn't even aware of the city streets and lights as they glided through London. They could have been transported to another planet. She was only aware of herself as some very primal feminine being, and of Andreas as her masculine counterpart.

She saw Andreas's head dip down, felt his hot breath feather over an almost painfully tight nipple before his mouth closed around it. Siena sank back against the seat, every bone in her body melting at the exquisite tugging sensation that seemed to connect directly to where a pulse throbbed between her legs.

As if reading her mind, Andreas moved his hand under her dress and up her legs, pushing them apart. She was helpless to resist as he expertly pulled down the bodice of her dress completely and bared her other breast, to which he administered the same torture.

Everything was coalescing within Siena, building to some elusive crescendo of tension. Her hips were rolling and one of her hands was in Andreas's hair, fingers tangling in silken strands as she held him to her breast. Her other hand was clenched tight, and an ache of gigantic proportions was growing between her thighs.

Andreas's long fingers had found her panties and he was tugging them down over her hips. Siena was mindless, wanting Andreas to alleviate this exquisite tension inside her. Her hips lifted and he slid the black lace down her legs, over her feet in their vertiginous heels and off completely.

And then Andreas's mouth left her breast and he straightened up. It took a second for Siena to register that he was just looking at her. Her breasts were bared and throbbing slightly, wet from his mouth and heaving with her laboured breath. Her dress was hiked up almost to her waist and her legs were parted. She saw her flimsy lace panties dangle from his fingers, and then he put them in the pocket of his jacket.

Siena's tongue felt thick. 'What are you doing?'

It was only then that she realised how pristine Andreas looked in his jacket and tie, barely a hair out of place. Far too belatedly she scrabbled with numb hands to pull her dress up over her breasts and down over her thighs.

'I'm making sure there's no delay once we get inside.'

Inside. It was only then that Siena became aware that they were outside his apartment building and the young valet was approaching the door of the car. Siena felt Andreas push her forward slightly, the brush of his fingers against her back as he pulled her zip up. Then he was handing her her wrap and the door was opened.

By the time she was out in the cool air she was incandescent with rage—not only at Andreas, but at herself for being so weak. When Andreas touched her back to guide her into the building she jerked away from him. She all but ran to the door and yanked it open before he could open it for her, making straight for the lift, punching the button with unnecessary force. Andreas was a tall dark presence beside her which she ignored.

When they stepped into the lift Siena moved to one corner and resolutely looked forward. To her absolute horror she could feel heat prickling at the backs of her eyes and her throat tightening. She willed down the emotion which had sprung up with every fibre of her being and swept out of the lift when the doors opened.

When Andreas joined her and opened the apartment door he had barely shut it behind him when she rounded on him, hands curled into fists.

'How *dare* you?'

Andreas looked so cool and composed and Siena was completely undone. Her hair was around her shoulders and she'd never felt more vulnerable.

'How dare I what, Siena? Kiss you?' His mouth twisted. 'How could I *not* have kissed you? Don't you know by now that I have a fatal attraction to your unique brand of remote aloofness?'

Siena could have laughed out loud. She'd never felt less remote or aloof. Right then she hated Andreas with a passion that scared her with its intensity.

She couldn't stop the words tumbling out. 'I hate you.'

'Be careful, Siena,' he mocked, 'Love is just the other side of hate, and we wouldn't want you falling for me, now, would we?'

Siena spluttered. '*Fall* for you? I couldn't think of anything less likely to happen.' Her words fell into a hole inside her and echoed painfully.

Siena lifted her chin, determined to get off that disturbing topic and claw back some control. 'I am not going to be ritually humiliated by you, whenever and wherever it takes your fancy.'

Andreas prowled closer and drew Siena's lace panties from his pocket, holding them up. Siena died a small death.

'It takes two to tango, Siena, and you were with me every second of the way back there. To be honest I hadn't expected you to be a back seat of the car kind of woman.'

Siena lifted her hand to grab her underwear but Andreas snatched them back out of her reach and then deposited the lacy scrap of material back into his pocket. Without realising he'd even moved, Siena found herself with her back against the main door of the apartment, her wrist held high in Andreas's hand, above her head. He was pressing against her and she could feel herself responding to that tall muscular length all over again. The heated insanity of what had happened came back in lurid Technicolor.

'Let me go,' Siena gritted out, desperately afraid of how susceptible she was.

He shook his head and his eyes glowed like dark jewels. 'Never. You're mine now, Siena, until I say so.'

And then he bent his head and his mouth found hers, and when she tried to turn her head away he only brought his free hand to her head and held her there, captive, as he kissed and stroked her weak resistance away with his clever tongue.

Siena was so full of turbulent emotions and sensations that it was almost a relief to give in to the sheer physicality of the moment. Here, with Andreas kissing her like this, she couldn't think. And she didn't want to.

When he finally released her hand she found herself, not pushing him away but clutching his shoulders, before find-

20% OFF*

with code
THANKSJUN

Visit www.millsandboon.co.uk
today to get this exclusive offer!

Ordering online is easy:

- 1000s of stories converted to eBook
- Big savings on titles you may have missed in store

Visit today and enter the code **THANKSJUN**
at the checkout today to receive **20% OFF**
your next purchase of books and eBooks*.
You could be settling down with your
favourite authors in no time!

MILLS &
BOON

JUN13

ing that her hand was sneaking underneath his jacket, to push it off.

Their mouths were fused together, tongues a tangle of heated lust, and when Andreas removed his hands so that he could shrug off his jacket Siena sought and found his bow-tie, undoing it so that she could open the top button of his shirt.

In some very dim place she told herself that she had a desire to see him as undone as she felt, but in truth she just had a growing need to see him naked.

Siena felt her zip being pulled down again, and it was almost a relief to have her breasts freed. Andreas's mouth and tongue was a potent memory. She wanted to feel him again. Her hands took his head, guiding him away from her mouth and down…

Only minutes after she'd stood in front of him, vowing she hated him, Andreas's mouth was on her breast and Siena was once again reduced to some writhing wanton. But her mind skittered weakly away from that anomaly.

Siena felt feverish. Her legs were weak. But she couldn't move. Andreas had straightened and was opening his shirt, ripping it off, and Siena's eyes grew huge and round as she took in his olive-skinned magnificence. Not an ounce of fat. All lean muscle. Flat brown nipples enticed her to lean forward and touch with her tongue, exploring his salty taste.

Andreas groaned softly and slid his hand into her hair. After a minute of her mouth torturing him with some pseudo-innocent touch she must have learned somewhere Andreas dragged her head back. Her mouth was open, she was panting slightly, and her eyes were wide and slumberous, pupils dilated. His erection thickened and with an impatient hand he undid his belt and zip, pulling down his trousers and his briefs with them. He had to have Siena *now*. He couldn't even move from this spot. He was aware that he was about to take her exactly as he'd fantasised five years ago, standing up, like some kind of feral animal. But he didn't care.

All he could see was that white-blonde hair tumbled over bare shoulders, her full round breasts, flushed and moist from his touch and his mouth. All he could think about was how her nipples had felt against his tongue—tight and puckered—the way she'd moaned when he touched her there.

Feeling ruthless, Andreas kicked away his clothes. He was naked now, and Siena's eyes grew bigger as she looked down his body, making him throb with a need to be inside her, thrusting up into the tight core of her body, seeking his release. Finally.

Cursing softly, having a flash of clarity at the last moment, Andreas reached down and pulled protection from his jacket, fumbling in a way he hadn't in a long time as he ripped it open and stroked the rubber along his length.

The scent of Siena's arousal hit him like a ton of bricks and, unable to stop himself, he fell to his knees before her, pulling her dress down all the way until it pooled at her feet in a tangle of chiffon and lace. Now she wore only her shoes, and Andreas removed them, hearing her husky, hesitant-sounding entreaty.

'Andreas...'

He ignored it.

His need was too strong to resist.

She was more than he could have ever imagined in his fantasies. Long slender limbs, pale all over. A triangle of blonde curls between her legs. Andreas knelt there and parted her thighs. He could feel her resistance but said gutturally, 'Let me taste you.'

After a second when her legs trembled so lightly he might have imagined it her resistance faltered and Andreas bared her to him, his mouth and tongue seeking and finding her essence, revelling in her sweetly musky smell and taste.

Her hand was in his hair, gripping tightly enough to be

painful, but it only fired him up even more. He could feel his erection strain against its rubber confinement between his legs and knew he couldn't wait. There would be more time to savour her later. But now he had to have her. He had to be buried so deep inside her that he would forget his own name.

Andreas surged up and just managed to catch Siena before she collapsed. He wrapped his arms around her, feeling her back arch into him, her breasts crushed against his chest.

'Wrap your legs around my waist,' he instructed roughly.

Siena put her arms around his neck, and then her legs were wrapped around his waist. Andreas hitched her up and rested her back against the door, so that it would take some of her weight, even though she felt as light as a feather.

Holding her with one arm, he reached down between them and ran his finger along her cleft. *She was so wet.* It nearly undid him there and then. He spread his legs and positioned himself, taking himself in his hand and guiding the head of his erection to those moist folds of flesh.

Andreas forced himself to curb the desire to thrust so far and so deep he'd find instant release. He was more than that. He wouldn't let her do this to him. He found her mouth and braced himself, before thrusting up and into the giving wet clasp of her body.

He felt her open-mouthed gasp of surprise before he registered that he'd felt an impediment to his movement. Sweat broke out on his brow. He drew away and looked at Siena, every nerve and muscle protesting at this interruption.

'What...?'

Siena was pale, and the unmistakable light of shock shone in her eyes. Stripped bare of that hazy pleasure he'd seen a moment ago. He flexed his buttocks and saw her wince as he moved a bit deeper. Her arms tightened around his neck. Andreas felt something cold prickle at his neck. It couldn't be possible... The information simply wouldn't compute...

He spoke out loud. 'You can't be…'

Siena was biting her lip now, and Andreas saw the sheen of moisture in her eyes. It was as if a two-ton lorry had crashed into his chest. He started to withdraw, but as he did he saw that moisture fade and a light of determination come into those glorious eyes.

She tightened her legs around his waist. 'No.' Her voice sounded raw. 'Don't stop.'

It hurt to breathe, but Andreas managed to get out, 'I'll hurt you…if we move—'

'No.' Siena's legs tightened even more. 'We do this. Here. Now. Just the way you said you wanted to five years ago…'

Andreas's brain felt as if it would explode. He was caught between heaven and hell. Siena's musky scent was all around him, her body clasped him, but not in the way he knew it could. He cried out for release.

And there was something so…*determined* about her. The fact that she was still a virgin was too much to process right now.

Andreas gave in. 'Try to relax your muscles…it'll be easier…'

He could see how she concentrated and he felt her body allowing him to go deeper. He all but groaned out loud at the exquisite sensation. She was so tight around him, almost painfully tight.

Moving her slightly, he bent his head and drew one taut nipple into his mouth, rolling it, sucking it back to life. He could feel what it did to Siena when her body relaxed even more, and with an exploratory move Andreas thrust a little higher. She hitched in a breath but he could sense that it wasn't a breath of pain. It was a breath of awareness.

When he lifted his head to look at her again she was not pale any more. She was flushed, biting her lip again. Slowly he withdrew from her body and then thrust back in, going even deeper this time.

Her hips twitched against his. She was breathing heavily now, saying almost against her will, 'I feel so full...'

'I know...just let me...trust me...it'll ease.'

Andreas was surprised he could string a sentence together. His world was reduced to this moment, this woman, this inexorable slide of his body in and out of hers. His passage was becoming easier and sweeter with every second. Siena's head fell back against the door and he could see her eyes closing.

Andreas put his hand to her chin and tugged it down. 'Look at me...Siena.'

She opened her eyes and they were feverish. With a feeling of triumph Andreas felt the ripples of her body around his as the onset of her orgasm approached. Ruthlessly he held his own desperate need for release at bay and pushed her higher and higher, seeing how her eyes widened, her cheeks flushed deep red. Her lips were engorged with blood. Her breasts were flushed, nipples like tight berries.

Somewhere in his head a voice crowed, *She's undone.* But it barely broke through Andreas's single-minded need to drive her over the edge. And when she fell it was spectacular. Her eyes grew even wider. She stopped breathing. Her whole body grew as taut as a string on a bow and then he saw the moment she fell and felt her body clench so tightly around his in waves of spasms that he was helpless except to allow his own release to finally break free.

He could do nothing but close his eyes and bury his head in her breast. Their laboured breathing sounded harsh in the silence of the foyer. His body pulsed within hers minutely. He felt her grip around his neck grow slack as if she couldn't hold on any more.

Eventually Andreas found some strength from somewhere and straightened. Siena was avoiding his eyes now, and she winced slightly as he pulled free and helped her to stand. Their clothes were strewn around them in chaotic abandon, but she still wore the necklace and bracelet.

Andreas had a sudden visceral need to take the jewellery off Siena. It was a reminder that wasn't welcome now. He undid the clasp of the necklace, letting it fall heavily into his hand, and then the bracelet. They clinked together with a hollow sound.

The sound of the jewellery knocking together seemed to resonate deep within Siena. Avoiding looking at Andreas, she bent down to pick up her dress, holding it against her like a very ineffectual shield. Resounding in her head with crystal clarity was the fact that she'd just lost her virginity to this man while standing up, against the door of his apartment.

She could remember the moment when she'd thought he was about to pull away, perhaps to take her into the bedroom. There'd been a look in his eyes that had threatened to shatter something inside her. And then the memory of that dawn morning in Paris, when Andreas had admitted that he'd wanted to take her up against the wall of the dressing room had rushed back.

Siena had seized on it and fought against the pull to make this easier...to be taken to surroundings more conducive for making love for the first time. Because this was not about romance.

She didn't want to think of the deeply disturbing emotion which had surged the moment he'd joined their bodies. That had made her feel weak and tender.

'*Theos*, Siena...' Andreas rasped. 'You were a virgin. Why didn't you tell me?'

She looked at Andreas and paled when she saw the look on his face, relieved to see that he'd pulled on his trousers. She couldn't handle him naked. Desperate to convince him it meant nothing, so that she could consider what it *did* mean in a private space on her own, she shrugged. 'It's no big deal. I was a virgin and now I'm not.'

Andreas's mouth twisted. 'So your father really was going to offer you up to a crusty blue-blooded relic like some virginal sacrifice?'

Siena's chest tightened. That was exactly what he'd planned. 'Yes,' she whispered, her bravado slipping. 'Something like that.'

Andreas cursed and Siena tried to avoid looking at his bare chest. It reminded her of how it had felt, crushed against her breasts.

'You should have told me, Siena…' he grated. 'If I'd even suspected you were innocent I'd have gone slower…been more gentle.'

'I'm fine,' Siena muttered, picking up her shoes, still avoiding looking at Andreas.

The air around them smelled of something unfamiliar but heady. *Sex.* Siena was too overwhelmed even to acknowledge that after the initial pain it had transcended anything she might have imagined.

She saw Andreas's bare feet come into her line of vision and gulped. As his finger tipped up her chin her eyes moved up and took in the fact that his top button was open, revealing that tantalising line of hair which led down— Her gaze landed on his face.

She felt the urge to strike first and said, 'Don't look so shocked just because I was a virgin, Andreas.'

He was angry, eyes blazing now. 'If I'd known I would never have taken you like that…'

'Why?' she taunted. 'It's exactly how you wanted to take me before—I didn't want to deny you the chance to fulfil your fantasy.'

Siena heard the words but wasn't really sure where on earth

the nerve to say them was coming from. She saw Andreas's face turn expressionless, shuttered. He took his hand away and stepped back, making Siena feel bereft.

'You should have a bath. You're likely to be sore.'

Siena was a lot more intimidated by this cool specimen than the anger Andreas had just displayed. The idea that he might have cared enough about her innocence to make it a more pleasurable experience was…

Before she could say anything else that might betray her, Siena fled.

Andreas watched Siena retreat and cursed silently. He'd expected that after making love to her, *finally,* he would be feeling a whole lot more sated and at peace. It was laughable. He'd never felt less sated and at peace. He wanted her again—*now.* Wanted to taste that lush, mutinous mouth, to make her eyes widen with desire again. Wanted to watch her tumble over the edge and feel her body clamp around his with those spasms of orgasm.

Andreas ran a hand through his hair impatiently and then bent to pick up the rest of his own clothes. Under the stinging hot needles of his shower a few minutes later he cursed again, volubly. He certainly hadn't intended on mauling Siena in the back of his car, but by the time they'd been pulling up outside his apartment and he'd realised what he was doing he'd had her panties in his hand, ready to take her there and then in the back seat.

From some distant area of his brain he'd managed to find something to mutter to make it sound as if he'd fully intended divesting her of her underwear so that they could continue where they left off as soon as as they were in a private space. Outside the car, though, she'd all but spat at him—and could he blame her? He'd never been so unrestrained with a woman.

He should have remembered that evening in Paris. Remembered how she was capable of making him lose all sense of civility. But when they'd danced in that hotel… Andreas had been sorely tempted to drag her into the lobby, demand a suite and take her upstairs right there. It was little wonder he'd been unable to resist touching her in the back of the car… she'd been melting into him like his hottest fantasy and he'd been lost.

Andreas switched off his shower with a curt flick of his wrist. *Siena had been a virgin.* He looked at himself in the mirror and saw how fiercely his eyes glittered.

It was the one thing he had not expected in a million years. A lot of his bitterness about what had happened in Paris had centered around the belief that Siena had knowingly seduced him because she was bored…and experienced. But she'd been a virgin. And what virgin got hot and heavy with a hotel duty manager? He knew damn well that if they hadn't been interrupted he would have discovered her innocence that night.

He recalled her pale face when she'd bumped into him the following morning. The way she'd looked when he'd told her how he should have taken her up against the wall of the dressing room. He'd said that because he'd felt like such a fool. Because he'd felt exposed, betrayed. Because he'd believed she was experienced, like all those other scarily worldly-wise debutantes.

The irony of it was Siena had been the real deal. Probably the only one there. And how in hell had she stayed a virgin till now? Andreas wanted to smash something with his fist.

He heard a faint noise from outside his bathroom and hitched a towel around his waist before going out. Siena was standing in the centre of the room, in a voluminous towelling robe, hair damp, and his body reacted instantaneously.

His recent unwelcome revelations made Andreas say curtly, 'Yes?'

He saw how Siena tensed and it only made him want to snarl more—but not at her. At himself.

'I just want you to know that it didn't mean anything…the

fact that you were my…first. And you're right, I should have told you. But I thought…'

Andreas saw her falter and bite her lip for a second. She looked almost unbelievably vulnerable. Then she went on, 'I thought you wouldn't notice, I didn't realise it would be so… obvious.'

Siena wanted the ground to swallow her whole and she looked down.

For a long moment nothing happened, and then Andreas conceded, 'It might not have been obvious to some men… but I knew.'

Siena flushed. She could imagine the kind of man her father would have wanted her to marry—some old lecher from the Italian Middle Ages—and just how that scenario might have played out.

She stubbed her toe against the luxurious carpet of his bedroom. 'Yes, well, I just wanted to assure you that it doesn't change anything.'

Siena looked up warily, very aware of Andreas's naked chest and long powerful legs. The excuse for a towel that barely covered his intense masculinity. Unbelievably, Siena could feel herself clench inwardly at the thought of how he'd surged up and into her…how it had felt when he'd slid in and out, taking her higher and higher.

Too late she realised her mistake in coming here like this and turned to leave, but quick as a flash Andreas inserted himself between her and the door.

'Where do you think you're going?'

Siena gulped. 'To my room. To bed.'

Andreas smiled and it was wicked. 'There's a perfectly good bed here.'

Siena blanched. As responsive as her body was proving to be, she didn't in all honesty think she could take a repeat so soon. She'd stung when she'd lowered herself into the bath and she ached all over.

Reading her mind, Andreas said, 'Don't worry, I think it's too soon—but there are other ways of achieving the same result.'

He took Siena by the hand and led her unresisting—much to her disgust—to the bed. He sat down and pulled her between his legs. His towel parted and when Siena looked down she could see the dark thatch of hair and his body stirring and hardening.

Andreas was undoing her robe and then pulling it open. Siena felt absurdly shy and tried to stop him, but he was too strong. It was off her shoulders, falling down her arms to the ground, and she was naked.

Andreas's gaze was fixed on her breasts and Siena could feel them grow, the tips hardening, tingling. She wanted to groan. How could she be so affected when he just looked at her?

With his hands clamped around her waist, Andreas brought her even closer and lavished her breasts with attention, licking and suckling until Siena wanted to cry out. The first time round it had all been happening so fast she hadn't had a chance to draw breath, drowning in sensations before she could really register them.

Now Andreas was conducting a slow, sensual torture, and Siena found it almost overwhelming. With a smooth move he caught her just as her legs threatened to buckle and laid her on the bed. He whipped aside his towel so that he was naked.

Siena said brokenly, 'I thought you said—'

He put a finger to her mouth and said, 'Shh, I did.'

Siena felt something scary erupt in her chest, because in that moment she realised that she trusted Andreas. He wouldn't hurt her, or push her further than she could go. But now his mouth was on hers and his hands were moulding and cupping her breasts and Siena gave up any coherent thought.

By the time his hand reached between her legs and sought where she felt so hot and wet Siena's hips were rolling impatiently. She wanted Andreas to take her again, soreness be damned. But he wouldn't.

Almost crying with frustration, she felt him move down her body and replace that hand with his mouth. He'd touched her like this before, but now it felt much more intimate. Siena was aware of how wanton she must look—legs stretched apart, hands clutching at Andreas's head, breathing fast, heart thumping painfully.

Andreas found her sensitised clitoris and flicked it with his tongue, while thrusting two fingers into her clasping body. *This* was what Siena wanted and needed. Her back arched and her hips all but lifted off the bed as she became some primal being, focused solely on Andreas's mouth and fingers as they made that tension within her coil so tight that she shouted out as he finally tipped her over the edge.

Siena seemed to float for a long time on a blissful haze of sated lethargy before she opened her eyes and realised that Andreas was lowering her into her own bed and pulling the covers over her. He'd carried her here, after pleasuring her senseless.

Siena quickly clamped her eyes shut again, not wanting to see the expression on his face and not liking how ambiguous her feelings were about his putting her back in her own bed. Eventually she heard his footfall and the sound of her door clicking shut. Her eyes opened again, seeing nothing for a moment in the darkened gloom.

Her whole body tingled and hummed with pleasure…and yet Andreas hadn't sought his own release. Siena turned over and looked unseeingly into the dark. She had no frame of reference for this kind of a relationship, but she hadn't expected Andreas to be a selfless lover.

Her head felt tangled and jumbled. She'd somehow naïvely expected that a physical relationship with Andreas would be something she could ultimately rise above, remain immune to, even if she fell apart slightly. She felt anything but immune now. She felt as if she'd been turned inside out and reconfigured and—terrifyingly—she wasn't sure if she even knew who she was any more.

CHAPTER SEVEN

THE FOLLOWING DAY, Siena was in one of Andreas's chauffeur-driven cars, being transported to a private airfield. She'd found a cheerful Mrs Bright in the kitchen that morning, and she had directed Siena's attention to a note left for her by Andreas.

Siena had been inordinately relieved not to have to face him again so soon. She'd read the note.

I have a meeting in Paris tomorrow morning. We will spend tonight there and go to the opera this evening. Pack accordingly and be ready to leave at three p.m.
Andreas

Siena could see that they were approaching the airfield now, and felt nervous at the thought of confronting Andreas again after he'd explored her body with such thorough intimacy and then deposited her back in her bed like an unwelcome visitor.

They swept in through wide gates and Siena could see a small Lear jet and a sleek silver sports car nearby. Andreas was taking out a small case and suit bag. Her belly swooped. He looked so tall and handsome. Intimidatingly so. Especially now that she knew the barely leashed power of the body underneath that suit.

The car stopped and Siena saw Andreas register it and straighten up. He looked intense, serious, and her nervous flutters increased. She had no experience of how to handle this situation. She smoothed her hand down her dress, feeling vulnerable now when she thought of how she'd chosen it over more casual clothes, how carefully she'd chosen a dress for the evening, along with the ubiquitous jewelry Andreas would expect her to wear. Because, after all, an inner voice reminded her, she'd demanded it.

Andreas watched Siena emerge from the back of the car and was glad he wore sunglasses which would hide the flare of lust in his eyes. She was wearing a champagne-coloured silk shirt dress, cinched in around her waist with a wide gold belt. The buttons were open, giving just enough of a hint of cleavage, and her hair was tumbled around her shoulders in golden abandon.

Her legs were long and bare, flat gold gladiator-style sandals on her feet. She looked effortlessly *un*-put-together in the way that only women wearing the best clothes could. The knowledge made him reel again: she was here and she was his. More irrevocably his than he'd ever imagined. But even now, much to his chagrin, he couldn't seem to drum up that sense of triumph. It was more of a restless need. As if he'd never get enough of her. It made him very nervous.

Andreas wanted to rip open the buttons of that dress and take her right there, standing against the car. *Like you took her against the door of your apartment last night?* Shame washed through him as he recalled the heated insanity of that coupling. The fact of her innocence. And the fact that while he'd managed to restrain himself from making love to her again before she was ready he'd had to touch her again.

Andreas cursed. This woman had made him useless for the whole day. He'd lost his train of thought in meetings and his assistant Becky had looked at him strangely when he'd left his office. He didn't need her to tell him that his usual cool, organised self had deserted him.

Before he could dwell on the disturbing side-effects of having Siena in his life and in his bed, Andreas strode forward and let an attendant take his things before taking Siena's bag in his hand.

And then, because once he came close to her and her scent hit his nostrils he was unable not to, he wrapped his other hand around her neck and pulled her close, settling a hot, swift kiss to her mouth. When he felt momentary hesitation give way to melting, his body hardened.

He drew back and without saying a word took her hand and led her up into the plane.

By the time they'd landed in Paris and were driving into the city centre Siena was feeling even more on edge. Andreas had largely ignored her for the flight, apart from one brief conversation. She wondered if this was what he did: ignored his lovers once he'd taken them to bed?

She'd been completely unprepared for that swift but incendiary kiss by the plane. It had unsettled her for the entire journey, making her nerve-ends tingle. Andreas had appeared unaffected, though, concentrating on his laptop with a frown between his brows and conducting a lengthy business discussion in Spanish. Siena could understand Spanish, as it had been one of her languages at finishing school, and she'd been surprised to hear him discussing the fate of hotel workers in a small hotel he'd just acquired in Mexico.

He'd said, 'That area is challenged enough as it is. I won't have those people struggling to find new jobs when I'm going to need their experience when the new hotel opens. I want you to offer them retainers, or help find them alternative employment until the work on the new hotel is finished.'

He clearly hadn't liked whatever the person on the other end of the phone had said, and had replied curtly, 'Well, that's why you work for me, Lucas, and not the other way around.'

Andreas had caught her looking at him as he'd terminated the conversation, and had raised a brow. She'd flushed and said, 'I'm the first to admit that I don't know much about business, but surely that isn't exactly good financial sense?'

Andreas had settled back in his seat, a small smile curving that sensual mouth. 'You agree with my field manager? And why not? You're right. It's not good financial sense. But the fact is that this small town in Mexico is where my benefactor and mentor came from. When I moved to New York I worked in a hotel for Ruben Carro. He liked me, saw that I had potential, and essentially groomed me to take over from him.

'He had no family or heirs, and unbeknown to me had an inoperable brain tumour. I think he felt an affinity with me, arriving from Europe, penniless. He'd come from Mexico as an impoverished worker. Both his parents were killed trying to get across the border. When he died he left everything to me with the proviso that I continue his name and that I do something to help improve his home town. He left a substantial part of his fortune to be used to that end. Buying this hotel is just the first step. There are further plans to develop the infrastructure and employment opportunities.'

Siena had felt a little shaky hearing all of this. She'd heard of the legendary billionaire hotelier Carro. 'That's a very ambitious project.'

Andreas had smiled. 'I'm a very ambitious man.'

'That's why your hotel chain is known as Xenakis-Carro? After him?'

An unmistakable look of pride had crossed Andreas's face. He'd nodded. 'I'm proud to be associated with his name. He was a good man and he offered me the opportunity of a lifetime. It's the least I can do to continue his legacy.'

Andreas had turned away then, back to his work, and the knowledge had sat heavily in Siena's belly. Clearly the newspaper reports about his business ethics had been wrong, and yet Andreas hadn't cared enough to defend himself when she'd slung that slur his way.

Siena's focus came back to the present now, as the familiar lines of the Champs-Elysées unfolded before them. Dusk was settling over the iconic city and Siena felt tense. She'd always loved Paris. Until the debutante ball. Until that evening. Since then, coming back here had been fraught with painful reminders of her own naïvety and what she'd done. And never more so than now, when she shared a car with the very man who was at the centre of those memories and emotions.

He was looking out of his window and seemed remote. Was he remembering too? Hating her even more? Siena shivered slightly. They were drawing around to the front of the huge glittering façade of a hotel, and Siena only realised where they were when they came to a smooth halt.

She looked at Andreas, who was regarding her coolly from the other side of the car. 'Is this some kind of a sick joke? Returning to the scene of the crime?'

Andreas's mouth tightened, and then he answered far too equably, 'Not at all, Siena. I don't play games like that. We've come here merely because it's impractical to go to another hotel when I own this one.'

Shock hit Siena and she looked out again at the stunning façade of the world-famous Paris hotel where the debutante ball was still held every year. She was aware of Andreas getting out of his side of the car and then he was opening her door. She looked up at him and suddenly, despite her shock, her breath got stuck in her throat and she saw only him, silhouetted against the dusk. He had never looked more gorgeous, or more dark and threatening with his stern visage. Images of the previous night slammed into her. She felt hot deep down inside her, where secret muscles clenched.

He put out a hand and said imperiously, 'Come.'

Siena fought the childish urge to cross her arms and say

stubbornly *no*. But eventually she put her hand into Andreas's and stepped out. He kept a tight hold of it as they walked into the hotel with much bowing and scraping from the staff.

Siena was surprised to see that the hotel had undergone a very beautiful overhaul since she'd seen it last. Gone was the rather over-fussy atmosphere. It felt lighter, younger, yet still oozed elegance and timeless wealth. This, Siena guessed, must be one of the reasons Andreas had become so successful in such a dizzyingly small amount of time.

Andreas was talking briefly to someone who looked like a manager, and then he was walking forward again without even a glance back to Siena. His hand was still tight around hers. A lift set apart from the others was waiting with open doors.

They stepped in and an attendant greeted them politely before pressing the one button. Siena was beginning to feel claustrophobic in the familiar surroundings, and tried to pull her hand free of Andreas's. He turned to look at her and only gripped hers tighter. This silent battle of wills went on behind the attendant, who was looking resolutely forward, avoiding eye contact.

After what seemed like aeons the lift came to a halt and the doors opened. Andreas said *merci* to the attendant and then they were stepping straight into what could only be described as a shining palace of golds and creams, with acres of soft cream carpet, parquet floors with faded oriental rugs, and floor-to-ceiling French doors and windows. Outside the Place de la Concorde was spectacularly lit up like a golden beacon.

Siena forgot herself for a moment, and only came back into the room when she realised that Andreas had finally let her hand go and was striding into the main drawing room, shucking off his suit jacket and dropping it into a nearby chair.

Everything that had brought her here to this moment—the fact that she had slept with this man and so blithely given him her innocence, his cool demeanour since she'd seen him again today—all combined now to make her feel very prickly and unsure of herself.

He had his back to her, hands on his hips, and she remarked caustically, 'So, you bought the hotel where you were once a lowly assistant manager because this is where you've always had the fantasy of bedding the debutante who got you sacked—is that it?'

Slowly Andreas turned around and Siena steeled herself. His hand came up to his slim silver-grey tie and long fingers undid it. He opened the top buttons of his shirt and just looked at her with a burning intensity before saying quietly, 'You regard yourself very highly if you think I did all that just so I might one day get you into bed seven floors above where you once teased me because you were a spoilt little socialite who got bored between her main course and dessert.'

Siena flushed at his rebuke. She knew what she'd said was grossly unfair, but if Andreas came too close she might shatter completely. Once again the knowledge that he wouldn't welcome the truth of that night washed through her with a sense of futility. Even if he did choose to believe her it would mercilessly expose her and her sister to his far too cynical judgement.

He crossed the space between them and Siena's breath caught in her throat. His eyes were narrowed on her. Instinctively Siena took a step back, panic and something much more treacherously exciting rising from her gut.

'Oh, no.' Andreas shook his head and reached for her with strong hands, wrapping them around her waist. 'We have some time before going to the opera and I know exactly how to spend it.'

Breath was a strangled bird in Siena's throat as Andreas blocked out everything behind him and bent his head, slanting that wicked hot mouth over hers. As predictable as the inclement English weather her body fizzed and simmered. Blood rushed to every nerve-point and to all parts of her body, en-gorging them, making them tight and sensitive.

It felt as if he was devouring her, sucking her under to some dark wicked place where all she wanted was to feel his mouth on hers. Siena wrapped her arms around Andreas's neck and her whole body strained to get closer to his. His tongue was rough and demanding, making Siena mewl a little when he took his mouth away to trail kisses over her jaw and down further.

Siena's spiteful little barb about his motives for buying the hotel had lodged in Andreas's gut, driving him to seek out physicality rather than think about it. But when he had to lift his head to draw in an unsteady breath and Siena's eyes stared up into his he couldn't escape…

He'd claimed otherwise, but he had to admit that once he'd known this hotel was up for grabs he'd had to have it—with a viscerality that went beyond mere business. But when he'd returned here, conquering owner, it hadn't felt as satisfying as he'd thought it would. It had felt somehow empty, hollow.

Andreas tried to force the unwelcome thoughts out of his head. He saw Siena's slightly swollen lips and flushed cheeks, felt her breasts rise and fall against his chest with her breath. Something caught his eye and he looked down to see that the only piece of jewellery she wore was the simple gold birdcage necklace. For some reason it made him unaccountably nervous. As if there was some hidden message he wasn't getting. He wasn't sure he wanted to get it.

He touched the necklace with a finger. 'I hope you've brought something more substantial than this to wear?'

Siena flushed and avoided his eyes. 'Of course.'

Her voice sounded husky, and just like that it pushed Andreas over the brink of control. With a smooth, effortless move he lifted Siena into his arms and strode to the master bedroom. She gave a little squeal and her arms tightened around him.

'This time—' he was grim '—we'll make it to the bedroom.'

When Siena woke a couple of hours later it was to feel fingers running up and down her bare back, along the indentations of her spine. It was delicious, and yet she felt as if she would never be able to open her eyes again. She frowned and made some incoherent mumble, distantly aware of pleasurable aches and sensations in her body, a faint tingling.

'Come on…we don't have much time to get ready.'

Siena's eyes snapped open when she heard that deep dark voice. Andreas was sitting on the edge of the bed in nothing but a small towel, smelling clean and fresh, his hair damp. He'd just had a shower. Siena was instantly awake.

He stood up, and she couldn't help but watch his sheer leonine grace as he unselfconsciously dropped the towel and went to the wardrobe to look for clothes. Siena averted her eyes. She still felt shellshocked by what had just happened. The way Andreas had stripped her bare, laid her on the bed and proceeded to explore her entire body with a thoroughness that had had her gasping, pleading and begging. Like some wanton stranger.

When he'd finally surged between her legs it had been all she could do not to explode right then, and Andreas had been a master of torture, bringing her close to the brink but never over…until she had been crying genuine tears of frustration. She could still feel them now, slightly sticky on her face. She hated that feeling of being a slave to his touch.

Humiliation washed through her and she cursed her relative innocence, not liking the thought of other, more proficient lovers who undoubtedly drove *him* over the edge.

After all, hadn't he specified that he expected her to be an

ABBY GREEN   119

inventive lover? Except when he touched her any semblance
of thought went out of the window and she could only feel.

Realising that she was still lying there, naked and moon-
ing, Siena sat up and took advantage of Andreas disappear-
ing into the bathroom to jump out and pull on her dress again,
covering up. She noticed that one or two buttons were missing
and blushed when she thought of Andreas's big hands, fumbling until he'd become irritated and yanked it open. A small
glow of pleasure infused her. Perhaps he wasn't as insouci-
ant as she thought?

Andreas reappeared, and Siena avoided looking at him
buttoning his shirt and scooted into the bathroom, closing
the door behind her. She rested with her back against it for a
moment, breathing in his provocative scent, then closed her
eyes and tried to convince herself that she could get through
this week and emerge at the other end unscathed and intact.

Andreas heard the shower running and imagined the water
running in rivulets over Siena's breasts and body. Arousal was
instant and Andreas cursed, gave up trying to close a cufflink
as if that was the problem.

He closed his eyes, but all he saw was how Siena had
looked lying face down in the bed moments before, naked,
arms stretched out, the curve of her breast visible. That stunning face looked somehow very innocent and young in repose,
her mouth a soft moue.

Making love to her this time had had none of the madness
of last night, but a different kind of insanity. Sliding into her
body had felt disturbing—as if he was touching a part of himself that was buried deep. He'd never lost himself so much
while making love to a woman that he literally became some
kind of primal animal, able only to obey his body's commands.

He'd expected that after making love to her he'd feel a
steady beat of triumph. After all, this was exactly what he'd

envisaged. Siena, naked and undone on his bed. Underneath him, begging for release.

She'd cried just now, when they'd made love. Sobbed for him to let her go, to stop torturing her. And he didn't like how her tears had affected him, making him feel guilty.

He'd been punishing her as much as himself, and when she'd finally tipped over the edge the strength of her orgasm had almost been too much for him to handle. He'd worn protection, but Andreas wouldn't have been surprised if the strength of his release had rendered it impotent.

In truth he hadn't expected sex to be this good with Siena. He'd expected her to be cool, distanced. Too concerned with how she looked to let herself be really sensual. Slightly uptight. And yet she was blowing his mind.

He heard the shower stop and suddenly felt a very uncustomary spurt of panic. He couldn't guarantee that if she walked out of that bathroom right now he wouldn't be able *not* to take her again and to hell with the opera.

Only one woman had ever entranced him so much that he'd deviated from his plans. And the fact that he'd willingly invited her back into his life was not a welcome reminder of his weakness.

Fear of keeping her father waiting had instilled within Siena an ability to get ready in record time, so she wasn't surprised when she saw Andreas's look of shock when she walked into the main salon a short time later.

The way his eyes widened sent a shaft of something hot to her belly. The dress was, after all, exquisite. It was one-shouldered, a swathe of dusky pink layers of chiffon, shot through with gold. It hugged her chest and waist and then fell to the floor. She'd pulled her hair up and wore a pair of large teardrop pink diamond earrings.

Feeling absurdly nervous, Siena asked, 'Will I do?'

Andreas smiled, but it looked harsh in the soft lighting of the palatial room. 'You know you'll do, Siena. I'm sure you don't need compliments from me.'

Siena flushed. She hadn't been searching for a compliment. Andreas looked more than stunning in a black tuxedo with a classic black bow-tie. His hair gleamed, still slightly damp, and his eyes looked like dark jewels.

He flicked a glance at his watch and then moved towards her.

'We should go or we'll miss the first half.'

Those nerves assailed her again when Andreas took her elbow in his hand, and Siena asked, 'Which opera is it?'

Andreas was opening the main door and he glanced at her. 'It's *La Bohème*.'

Siena couldn't stop the spontaneous rush of pleasure. 'That's my favourite opera.'

Dryly Andreas remarked as they got into the private lift, 'Mine too. Perhaps we have something in common after all.'

The rush of pleasure died. No doubt Andreas was alluding to the disparity in their upbringings. She didn't know much about his early life, but she knew it had been relatively humble.

Curious in a way she hadn't been before, Siena found herself asking when they were in the back of his car, 'Do you come from a big family?'

Andreas looked at her, but his face was in shadow. She could sense him tense at the question and wondered why.

Eventually he answered, 'I have five younger sisters and my parents.'

Siena felt her curiosity increase on hearing this. 'I didn't realise you came from such a big family. Are you close?'

She could make out his jaw tightening. More reluctance. Clearly he didn't want to talk about it. Siena confided nervously, 'It was just me and Serena. I always wondered what it would be like—' She broke off because she'd been about to say: *to have an older brother.* But of course she did have an older brother.

Andreas, as if seizing the opportunity to deflect attention, asked, 'What *what* would be like?'

Siena swallowed. 'Just…what it would have been like to have other siblings.'

Andreas arched a brow. 'More sisters for your father to parade like ice princesses?' Before Siena could react to that Andreas was saying curtly, 'My family is not up for discussion. We come from worlds apart, Siena, that's all you need to know.'

It was like a slap in the face. Siena sat back into the shadows and looked out of the window. That tiny glimpse into Andreas's life had intrigued her, but she berated herself now for showing an interest, and hated that her imagination was seizing on what it would have been like to grow up in a large family. How being an only son might have impacted Andreas, fed his ambition to succeed.

She didn't care, she told herself ruthlessly, as they pulled up outside the opera. A long line of beautifully dressed people were walking in ahead of them. Andreas came around to her door and held out his hand imperiously. Siena longed to be able to defy him but she thought of her only family: Serena, in a psychiatric unit in England, depending on her. She put her hand into Andreas's.

Three nights later Siena was standing in Andreas's London apartment, waiting for him to emerge from his room where he'd gone to get changed. She was already dressed and ready as Andreas had been delayed with work.

Since that evening in Paris things had cooled noticeably between them. Not, she had to admit, that they'd ever really been *warm.* Andreas had barely said another two words to her that night, and when they'd returned from the opera he'd told her he had to do some work and had disappeared into an office in the suite.

When she'd woken the next morning the bed beside her had been untouched, so Andreas must have slept somewhere else. Siena hadn't liked the feeling of insecurity that had gripped her as she'd waited for Andreas to finish his meetings that morning so they could return to London.

However, when they'd returned to London that evening Andreas had led her straight to his bed and made love to her with such intensity that she hadn't been able to move a muscle. Siena didn't like to think of how willingly she'd gone into his arms, or the sense of relief she'd felt. Was she so weak and pathetic after a lifetime of bullying by her father that she welcomed this treatment? She seized on the fact that soon she would be independent again, and that she'd gone into this arrangement very willingly for an end which justified the means.

The following day Andreas had exhibited the same cool, emotional distance, confirming for Siena that this was how it would be unless they were in bed. On one level she'd welcomed it. She didn't need Andreas to charm her, to pretend to something their relationship would never be.

On both evenings they'd gone out to functions. Last night had been a huge benefit for a charity that provided money for children injured in war-torn countries to be brought to Europe or the USA for medical treatment. It covered all their costs, including rehabilitation.

Siena had had tears in her eyes when a beautiful young Afghan woman had stood up to tell her story. She'd been shot because she'd spoken out about education as a teenager and this charity had transported her to America, where she'd received pioneering surgery and not only survived but thrived. She now worked for the UN.

It was only when the head of the charity had introduced the charity's patron and invited him up to speak that Siena had realised it was Andreas. She'd sat there, stunned, listening to him speak passionately about not letting the children of conflict suffer. She'd felt absurdly hurt that he hadn't told her of his involvement.

When he'd come back to the table, Siena had pushed down the hurt. 'What made you want to get involved in something like this?'

His stern expression had reminded Siena that she was straying off the path of being his mute and supplicant mistress, and in that moment she'd wanted to stand up and walk out. Only thinking of Serena had kept her where she was.

Eventually he'd said, 'A child in Mexico was caught in the crossfire between drug gangs. Ruben arranged for him to be brought to New York for treatment...unfortunately the child died, despite the doctors' best efforts. I have eight nieces and nephews and they take their safety and security completely for granted—which is their right. This child from Mexico... It opened my eyes. After he died I knew I wanted to do more...'

Siena had realised then that she could not cling onto any prejudice she'd had about the kind of man Andreas was now she'd met him again. He was not power-hungry and greedy. Or amoral.

Ignoring his silent instruction not to pursue this topic, Siena had asked, 'Do you want children?'

Andreas had looked at her and smiled mockingly, making Siena instantly regret her reckless question. She'd realised then that she'd asked it in a bid to pierce that cool control, because the last time they'd shared any meaningful dialogue it had been about his family.

'Why, Siena? Are you offering to be the mother of my children? So that you can bring them up to follow in your footsteps and tease men before letting them fall to the ground so hard that their whole world shatters? Maybe if we had a daughter we could call her Estella, after that great Dickensian heroine who beguiled and bewitched poor hapless Pip with her beauty only to crush him like a fly…'

She had been so shocked at this softly delivered attack that she'd put down her napkin and stood up, saying quietly, 'You're no Pip, Andreas, and you don't remember correctly. Estella was the victim.'

Siena had walked blindly to the bathroom and shut herself inside. She hadn't been able to stop the hot prickle of tears from overflowing. She'd been stunned at how hurt she felt, and at the mixture of guilt and shame that churned in her gut along with the awful image Andreas had just put in her head.

He could never know how cruel his words were. Her deepest, most fervent dream was some day to be part of the kind of family unit she'd never known.

She'd used to look out of her bedroom window in Florence to a park on the other side of the tiny *piazza* outside their *palazzo*. There she would see mothers and fathers and children. She'd seen love and affection and laughter and she'd ached with a physical pain to know what that would be like. To love and be loved. To have children and give them all the security and affection she'd never known… She'd never even realised until Andreas had uttered those words how badly she still wanted it.

When she'd felt composed enough to return Andreas had been waiting impatiently and they'd left. He'd looked at her in the dark shadows of the back of his car and Siena had instinctively recoiled, unable to bear the thought of him touching her when she felt so raw.

He'd said roughly, 'You say Estella was the victim? From where I'm sitting she looks remarkably robust.'

He'd reached for her then, and Siena had resisted with all the strength in her body, hating him with every fibre of her being. But with remorseless skill Andreas had slowly ground down her defences and her anger until desire burned hotter than anything else…

By the time they'd made it to the apartment she'd forgotten all about her hurt and had been thinking only about Andreas providing her with the release he could give her, like someone pathetically addicted to an illegal substance.

'We should go or we'll be late.'

Andrea's terse voice made Siena jump slightly. She'd been caught up in the memory. She turned around and wondered if she'd ever get used to the little shock of awe when she saw him in a tuxedo. Thinking of the previous evening and what had happened made Siena look down, hiding her gaze. She picked up her wrap and bag and for the first time could appreciate the armour of her shimmering black designer dress. The heavy weight of a diamond necklace at her throat, the earrings in her ears and the bracelet on her wrist would keep her anchored tonight. She couldn't afford to lose herself for a second. Or let him goad her.

If Andreas had a hint of her vulnerability he'd annihilate her.

CHAPTER EIGHT

ANDREAS WAS DRIVING them to the function in his sports car. It served the purpose of occupying his hands and his mind, so that he wasn't in danger of ravishing Siena in the confined space of the back of his chauffeur-driven car. He would not debase himself again by proving that he could not last a few minutes without touching her. He didn't want to think of the amount of times he'd almost made love to her in the back of that car.

It made him think of the other night and how he'd still had to touch her even when she'd detonated a small internal bomb with her question about whether or not he wanted children. He didn't want to remember how she'd looked when he'd likened her to Estella from *Great Expectations* not once, but twice. It had worked, though. He'd welcomed the anger sparking in her eyes. Far easier to deal with that than the look in her eyes when she'd asked her question so inoccuously.

Lovers had asked Andreas before if he wanted children, and in every case Andreas had looked at them coolly and mentally ended the affair with little or no regret. Siena had asked and he had felt a primal surge of something very proprietorial. Something very disturbing that *wasn't* an immediate and categoric rejection of what should be anathema to him. In that moment he'd felt exposed and reminded of his humiliation in Paris. Had Siena seen something he'd been unaware of?

Something that had told her it was okay to ask that question because one week would not be enough for him? Because inevitably he couldn't help but want more?

Andreas had felt like Pip then, from that great book. Chasing after an ever unattainable beauty. Forever destined to fall short. And so he'd lashed out. Had watched her pale and told himself she was acting.

He needed to maintain the distance he'd instigated in Paris. Too much had made him uneasy there and since: Siena's insight into why he'd bought that hotel, the hunger for her which only seemed to be growing stronger, not weaker, and the way she'd asked him about his family…making him remember what he'd worked so hard to avoid.

So much of Andreas's youthful rejection of his family had been brought into sharp focus after his humiliating rejection at her hands. He'd gone abroad with little or no warning, and he knew it had confused and upset his parents. They'd never really understood his hunger to succeed, how he'd had an irrational fear of not making it out of that small town—especially after Spiro had died.

Andreas reminded himself that this wasn't a relationship like any other. With other lovers Andreas made an effort, small-talked, was witty and charming. With Siena it was about settling a score, sating the fever in his blood, exorcising the demons. He conveniently blocked out the fact that he appeared to be no closer to his goal than he had been a few days ago…

A couple of hours later Siena was feeling pain in the balls of her feet from the high heels. She wondered what Andreas would say if he knew that, contrary to his opinion of her, she'd give her right arm never to go to one of these functions again. Just then a tall, very good-looking man with dark hair approached Andreas and the two men greeted each other warmly. Siena found herself transfixed by Andreas's wide smile. She'd seen it so rarely since they'd met again, and never directed at *her*.

He was introducing the stranger. 'This is Rafaele Falcone, of Falcone Industries. He's recently moved to London to extend his domination of the motor industry.'

Siena recognised the name of the iconic Italian car company and put her hand out. She smiled at the other man, who matched Andreas in height and build. He truly was sinfully gorgeous, with astonishing green eyes, and Siena had a fleeting moment of wishing he would have some effect on her which might prove that Andreas didn't dominate her every sense. But when their hands touched there was nothing—despite the fact that Rafaele held her hand for a split second longer than was necessary, with a smile that made Siena feel like apologising because its effect was wasted on her.

'If you find things getting dull with Xenakis, do give me a call.'

He was handing her a card, flirting outrageously, and Siena found herself smiling at his chutzpah with genuine amusement. She was reaching for the card out of politeness when it disappeared into Andreas's fingers. His arm had come around her waist and brought her to his side in a way that had her looking at him, bemused. He'd never claimed her like this in public before.

Rafaele Falcone was putting up his hands in a gesture of mock defeat and backing away. 'We'll talk soon, Xenakis, I'll be interested to hear how that deal goes, and I have a new car being launched next month that I think you'll like…'

His gaze encompassed Siena and she flushed, suddenly not liking the way he was all but telling her of his interest if she were not with Andreas. She wasn't really used to this kind of casual interplay. Her father had always been so protective.

When he'd turned and walked away Andreas let Siena go and turned to her. He was livid, and Siena took a step back.

'Don't even *think* about it.'

Siena was genuinely confused. 'Think about what?'

Andreas jerked his head in the direction of his departing friend. 'Falcone is off-limits.'

Rage filled Siena, and she knew it was coming from a dangerous place—more from Andreas's dogged coolness in the past few days than what he'd just said. His possessiveness made her feel something altogether much more disturbing.

'How dare you? When we're done I can do what I like, and I intend to. If I think that includes having a rampant affair with Rafaele Falcone then I'll be sure to give him a call.'

For a second Andreas looked so feral that Siena felt fear snake down her spine. He looked capable of violence.

'You're mine, Siena,' he growled. 'No one else's.'

She lashed back. 'One week, Xenakis. I'm yours for one week. You're the one who put a time limit on it.' Realisation hit her then, along with something very hollow. 'And that one week is up in two days—or have you come to enjoy my company so much that you'd forgotten? Perhaps you want more?'

Siena wasn't sure what was goading her when she said waspishly, 'If you're so concerned with keeping me out of other men's beds it's going to cost you a lot more than a few baubles.'

'So this is how you're funding yourself after our father's spectacular crash and burn? I shouldn't be surprised.'

It took long seconds before Siena realised that it wasn't Andreas who had spoken in his deep voice. It was another voice—one that rang the faintest of bells. She tore her eyes from Andreas and looked to her left. She felt the blood drain from her face.

Rocco DeMarco. Her brother.

Siena barely heard Andreas acknowledge him tersely, 'DeMarco.'

Her brother's dark brown eyes left Siena momentarily to

flick to Andreas, and he inclined his head slightly. 'Xenakis. I see that my little half-sister Siena has found a benefactor to keep her in the style to which she's accustomed.'

His resemblance to their father stunned her anew, as it had all those years before, and Siena wanted to weep with the ill-timing of this meeting. It was effortlessly confirming his worst opinion of her.

Faintly she said, 'You recognise me.' It wasn't a question.

Those dark eyes went back to her. His mouth curled. 'I followed the demise of our father in the press with great interest. You and your sister were featured prominently, but it would appear you've landed on your feet.'

Feeling weak, Siena said, 'This…it's not what it seems.'

Disgust was evident in Rocco's expression, ice in his eyes, and Siena felt an ache in her heart. He was her flesh and blood.

'Did you really think I would ever forget you? After you and Serena stepped over me like a piece of trash in the street? And as for our father… Tell me—have you heard from him?'

Siena shook her head, feeling sick. How could she explain here and now to this man that she hated her father as much as he did?

Just then a petite and very pretty red-haired woman joined Rocco, slipping her hand into his arm. The change in her brother was instantaneous as he drew her close and looked down at her, warmth and love shining from his eyes. When he looked back at Siena the ice returned and she shivered.

'This is my wife—Gracie. Gracie, I'd like you to meet Siena. My youngest half-sister.'

Siena watched the woman tense and a wary expression came into her kind hazel eyes. Clearly she understood the significance of this meeting. She held out a hand, though, and Siena forced herself to shake it, feeling sick. She only noticed then the other woman's very pregnant belly, and something sharp and poignant lanced her at the realisation that she might have a nephew or niece already.

Rocco looked at Andreas and said with deceptive lightness, 'I presume from your expression that Siena hasn't told you about our familial connection? Or about when I confronted our father and he knocked me to the ground as if I was nothing more than a dog in the street?'

'Rocco...'

Siena heard his wife speak reprovingly, but his face remained ice-cold.

Siena found herself appealing to the other woman instinctively, saying, 'I was only twelve. Things really weren't as they seemed.'

The compassion in his wife's eyes was too much for Siena. She pulled free of Andreas, whose expression she did not want to see, and all but ran from the room. The emotion blooming inside her was too much. Here was incontrovertible proof that she and Serena were on their own. She'd known very well that she couldn't go to their brother, but it was another thing to see it for certain, no matter how kind his wife looked.

She'd always harboured a secret fantasy that one day she might go to Rocco and explain about their lives. That truly they weren't all that different in the end...they had a common nemesis: *their father.*

Her throat burned as she tried to suppress the emotion, expecting Andreas's presence at any moment. He wouldn't stand for her running out like that. Not when she had a duty to fulfil by his side. Perhaps he'd be so disgusted by what he'd just learned that he'd be happy to see the back of her?

She heard his voice, cold behind her in the quiet part of the lobby she'd escaped to.

'Why didn't you tell me Rocco DeMarco was your half-brother?'

Siena didn't turn around, struggling to compose herself. 'It wasn't relevant.'

Andreas snorted indelicately. 'Not relevant? He's one of the most powerful financiers in the world.'

Siena turned then and looked up at Andreas, steeling herself for his expression. It was exactly as she'd feared: a mixture of disgust and confusion. Siena retreated into attack to hide her raw emotions. She shrugged minutely. 'As you can see he hates my guts, and my sister's. Why should I bother myself with my father's bastard son—born to a common prostitute?'

Siena's insides were lacerated at her words. It was the opposite of what she believed. After that day when he'd confronted their father Siena had used to dream of him returning in the dead of night to take her and Serena away with him. But there was no way she would reveal that to Andreas.

'Why, indeed?' Andreas said now, and looked at her strangely. And then he started walking away, towards the entrance.

Siena faltered for a moment and went after him, having to hurry to keep up. When it was clear he was asking for his car, she asked a little breathlessly, 'Don't you want to go back inside?'

Andreas glanced at her and said curtly, 'Rocco DeMarco and his wife are friends of mine. I won't have them feeling the need to leave just because you're with me. I told them we'd leave.'

Pain, sharp and intense, gripped Siena as the car pulled up beside them and the valet jumped out, handing Andreas the keys. Solicitous as ever, even when he despised her, he saw Siena into the car and walked around the bonnet. Siena had the bleakest sense of foreboding that this was it. And after a silent journey back to the apartment Andreas confirmed it.

Barely looking at her, he was in the act of removing his jacket and taking off his cufflinks when he said, 'I'll arrange for a security guard to take you to the jewellers in the morning. There you'll be able to get your money.'

Siena stood stock-still. The stark finality of his words seemed to drop somewhere between them and shatter on the floor.

Faintly, pathetically, she said, 'But...there's two days left.'

Andreas speared her with a cold look. 'Five days is enough for me.' His mouth twisted. 'Don't worry. I won't dock you any *payment*.'

His words seem to bounce off her. She was numb. Just like that he'd lifted her up and now he was dropping her from a height. And yet...what else had she expected?

Siena felt sick when she had to admit that on some very deep and secret level she'd imagined that Andreas might not despise her so utterly—but when had they ever had a chance to go beyond that?

He'd stonewalled any attempts she'd made to talk about personal things, or even non-personal things, and yet this evening she could remember a betraying flare of hope at seeing him so possessive when another man flirted with her.

But that had been purely male posturing. No doubt he'd be quite happy to see her in anyone else's arms when *he* was done with her. Which was now, Siena realised a little dazedly.

She hated herself for not feeling more relieved, and she felt humiliated. Because she had to acknowledge that, despite telling herself she was with Andreas for this week purely to help her sister, she knew it was a lie. She would have wanted Andreas no matter what. For herself. Because he'd always been her dark fantasy. He would only ever have wanted her in revenge, so she'd had to have him like this or not at all.

Using Serena had been a buffer—a device for fooling herself that she was somehow in control...

Siena felt cold inside. The only good thing that could come out of this now was the help she could give her sister. She would take this man's largesse and damn herself in his eyes for ever. She'd do it with a willing heart because she had no right ever to have imagined anything else.

Siena forced herself to move, to say something. 'Goodnight, then.' It couldn't be more apparent that Andreas would not touch her now if his life depended on it.

She was walking away when she heard him say, 'It's goodbye, Siena. I'll be gone in the morning. I leave for New York to work.'

Siena turned and a wave of emotion surged upwards. She couldn't stop the words tumbling out in spite of her best intentions to stay cool. 'I *am* sorry, Andreas. Really sorry for what happened…it wasn't my intention…'

And then, before she could say anything more, she fled.

Andreas looked at the empty space Siena had left behind, along with the most fragile scent, and wanted to storm after her, to whirl her around and demand to know what she'd meant by *'it wasn't my intention'*. He wanted to put her over his shoulder and take her to his bed one more time.

But it would not be enough, he realised. It would never be enough. His body burned with need. Even after that distasteful scene with her half-brother and the knowledge of what he'd been through.

Andreas had had no idea of their connection. But as Rocco had spoken he'd felt the man's pain and had all too well been able to imagine the scenario—the two precious blue-eyed heiresses stepping over their prone brother.

It had brought back all of his own anger and rage, far too easily forgotten in the heat of passion or when Siena looked at him with those huge blue eyes. He too had suffered at those hands.

Until she'd reminded him that a week was almost up he had forgotten. And that had sent shockwaves through his system—along with a knee-jerk impulse to negate it, to tell her he'd let her go when he was ready.

But he'd caught himself in time. He'd forgotten and she'd remembered, because *she* was counting each day and evaluating how much she'd take from him.

She'd made him jealous. He thought of the red haze of rage that had settled over his vision on seeing his friend Rafaele Falcone flirt with Siena. And how she'd smiled at him so guilelessly, as she'd once smiled at him… That was when the scales had finally fallen from Andreas's eyes, and he'd realised how in danger he was of becoming a slave to his desire for this woman—how, far from being exorcised, she was gaining a stronger hold over him.

Andreas castigated himself. He should never have looked for her. It had been a huge mistake. Tomorrow she would be gone and he *would* move on.

A month later, London.

Andreas stepped into his apartment, bone-weary. He'd extended his trip to New York, not liking to investigate why he'd wanted to avoid coming back to London too soon. Silence descended around him, telling him he was alone. He ignored the hollow sensation and put down his bag.

He walked into the main salon and a vision hit him right between the eyes of Siena as she'd turned to face him that last evening in her black dress. So perfect. So beautiful. Andreas cursed and quickly walked out again.

He went to the kitchen, but that only brought him back to the moment when he'd heard Mrs Bright clucking and explaining to Siena about the oven. Or how Siena had looked sitting in jeans and a T-shirt, eating a croissant with her fingers.

Telling himself he was being ridiculous, he went to her room and opened the door, almost steeling himself for her scent. It lingered only faintly, but it was enough to have heat building low in his pelvis. He cursed her ghostly presence again. He was about to walk out when he spotted something out of the corner of his eye and walked towards the dressing area.

He couldn't be certain, but it looked as if every single piece of clothing he'd bought her was still there, neatly hung up or folded away. The long pink chiffon gown. The black dress she'd worn that first night, which had ended up on the floor of the foyer as he'd taken her up against the front door with all the finesse of a rutting bull... Andreas flushed.

The clothes would have been worth a fortune, if she had felt inclined to sell them, but they were here. Something very alien gripped Andreas and he strode out and into his study. Already he could see the safe door open and all of the jewellery gone.

He didn't like his momentary suspicion that perhaps she'd left the jewellery too. Some last second attack of conscience, because... *Why?* he mocked himself. *Because she'd come to feel something for you?*

Andreas pushed aside the rogue thought, not liking how it made him break out in a cold sweat. He sat down and picked up his phone. He had to know for sure.

'Yes, Mr Xenakis. She came that morning, as you'd arranged, and handed back every item of jewellery. We exchanged it all for a very fair price. She was a pleasant young lady.'

Andreas did not want to get into a conversation about how Siena DePiero could turn on the charm when it suited her, and he was about to put the phone down when the man on the other end said, 'Actually...there was one item she wanted to keep. Ah... Let me see...'

He was clearly looking at some list, and Andreas bit down on his impatience. He really didn't want to hear about which emerald bracelet Siena had—

'Ah, yes. Here it is.'

The man interrupted his train of thought.

'She wanted to keep the gold birdcage necklace by Angel Parnassus, and she was very insistent that she pay for it out of her own money. Everything else was cashed.'

Andreas muttered his thanks and put the phone down. As soon as Siena had singled out that understated necklace it had made him nervous, and he didn't like to be reminded of that now—of that elusive sensation that he'd missed something.

With a curse, Andreas stood up and went to his room to change for the reception of a wedding that he was invited to that evening in one of his London hotels.

His brief interlude with Siena DePiero was over, and he didn't really care why she had wanted to hang onto some relatively inexpensive piece of gold. Nor did he want to dwell on the fact that she was out there, somewhere in the city, living off his money and undoubtedly seducing the next billionaire stupid enough to fall under her spell.

A sudden vivid image of her with Rafaele Falcone made Andreas feel as if something had just punched him in the gut, and he had to breathe deeply to ease the sensation.

Curse her to hell. He was done with her for good, and soon the bad taste left in his mouth would fade. If she was with Rafaele Falcone he was welcome to her.

Siena turned away from another group of wedding guests who had barely looked at her as they'd helped themselves to some of the *hors d'oeuvres* she was offering from a silver tray. She welcomed the anonymity. She'd had this job for two weeks now, and she knew how lucky she was to have found another job so easily.

Every penny that had come from the sale of the jewellery from Andreas had gone straight to cover Serena's fees. She'd spent an emotional afternoon with her sister, assuring her that she would be okay, and in that moment Siena had had no regrets about what she had done.

It was when she lay in bed at night, in a similarly dingy apartment to her last one, or took the bone-rattling bus journey to work every day that she felt acute regret for deceiving Andreas all over again. She'd never forget the way he'd looked at her that last evening, or the painful reunion with her brother. Something she hadn't yet divulged to Serena.

Siena was making a beeline towards another group of guests in their finery when one of the men turned slightly to speak to a man at his side. Siena stopped in her tracks just feet away. Her belly plummeted. It couldn't be. The universe couldn't be so cruel.

But apparently the universe *could* be that cruel. Andreas Xenakis glanced momentarily in her direction and Siena saw the shock of recognition cross his features.

She immediately turned on the spot and walked quickly away, assuring herself a little hysterically that he wouldn't have recognised her. He would thhink he was mistaken because he would have assumed she'd be on a yacht, sunning herself in the Mediterranean, spending the money she'd received.

But even as she thought that she knew it was too good to be true. A heavy hand fell on her shoulder and she was whirled around so fast that the tray flew out of her hands, landing upside down on the plush and very expensive carpet nearby.

Siena immediately jerked free and bent down to pick up the tray and limit the damage, terrified her stern boss might have seen. Andreas bent down too, and Siena hissed at him, hating the way her heart was threatening to jump free of her chest, 'Please just leave me alone. I can't afford to lose this job.'

'And why,' he asked with deceptive mildness, 'would that be, when only weeks ago you cashed in a small fortune? No one could have run through it that quickly.'

Siena finished putting the last of the ruined canapés on the tray and lifted it up again. She looked at Andreas and hated how shaky she felt. 'Just pretend you haven't seen me. *Please.* If I'd had any idea you'd be a guest here...'

'Mr Xenakis, is everything all right?'

'No, it's not all right,' Andreas snapped at Siena's boss, who blanched.

Siena went hot with embarrassment. People were looking at them now, interested in whatever it was that had taken Andreas Xenakis's attention. The sense of déjà-vu as Siena remembered how she'd first seen him again was not welcome.

Andreas took the tray out of Siena's hand and before she knew what was happening handed it to her boss, taking her hand. 'I'm sorry, but you'll have to do without her. She's resigning from her job.'

Siena gasped, 'No, I'm not! How dare you?' But her words were lost as Andreas all but dragged her through the throng of merry wedding guests. She tried to free herself but Andreas's grip was too tight.

He stopped suddenly and she almost careened into his back—only to hear him say to the tall dashing groom and his stunning bride, 'So sorry...something has come up. I wish you all the best.'

And then he was moving again.

Her face puce with mortification, Siena was forced to follow. When they were finally in the clear, in a relatively empty corridor, Siena broke free and stopped in her tracks. She was shaking with adrenalin and shock.

'How *dare* you just lose me my job like that?'

Andreas rounded on her, eyes blazing. Siena couldn't fail to react to his sheer masculine magnificence. His jaw was slightly stubbled and an insidious image slipped into her mind of him waking in bed with some new lover who had distracted him enough to persuade him back into bed. Something she'd never done. She'd never woken in his arms.

'Lose you your job?' he practically shouted. 'Why the hell are you working as a waitress again when you walked away with a small fortune in your pocket just a month ago?'

Siena opened her mouth and shut it again. What could she say? That she liked back-breaking work and being on her feet for eight hours solid at a stretch? Of course she didn't.

She just needed Andreas gone so that she could get on with trying to forget about him and all the tangled emotions he was responsible for. She folded her arms. 'It's none of your business.'

Andreas folded his arms too, as immovable as a large, intimidating statue. Siena knew with a flicker of trepidation that she'd never make him budge.

'You owe me an explanation, Siena.'

Siena shook her head, panic surging. 'No, I don't owe you anything.'

Andreas looked stern. 'Oh, yes, you do—and especially after this stunt.'

He reached for her hand again and started leading her down the corridor, away from the high society wedding. A sense of inevitability washed through Siena. She knew she hadn't a hope of resisting Andreas when he was like this.

To her dismay she realised that they were in one of his hotels when he went to the reception desk and she heard him demand the key for the Presidential Suite. Then they were in the lift and ascending to the top floor. He still had hold of her hand, and Siena didn't like the way her body was already reacting to his touch—her blood pooling hotly in her belly and fizzing through her veins.

When Andreas opened the door to an opulent-looking suite he led her in and only let her go when they were safely inside. Siena walked into the reception room. The lights of the Houses of Parliament shone from across the river in the gathering dusk.

She felt self-conscious in her uniform, which consisted of a black knee-length skirt, a white shirt and black bow-tie. Her hair was pulled back into a ponytail, face scrubbed free of make-up, and the only jewellery she wore was the gold bird-cage necklace she'd kept. It seemed to burn into her skin like a brand now, even though she'd actually used the last of her own money to pay for it.

She heard the sound of Andreas pouring himself a drink and turned around to find him handing her a small tumbler of Baileys. She was surprised that he'd remembered her favourite drink and took it in both hands, avoiding his eye.

'Sit down, Siena, before you fall down.' His tone was admonitory.

Siena looked around and saw a chair sitting at right angles to the couch. She sat down and took a tiny fortifying sip of her drink, feeling the smooth, creamy liquid slide down her throat.

Andreas went and stood with his back to her at the window and Siena regarded that broad back warily, her eyes dropping to his buttocks. Instantly she had a flashback to how it had felt to have him between her legs, thrusting so deep—

He turned around abruptly and she flushed.

'So, is it that you have some masochistic penchant for menial labour after a life of excess? Or perhaps you've acted completely out of character, had a fit of conscience and handed all the money over to a worthy charity? I want to know what you've done with my money, Siena. After all, it's not an inconsiderable sum…'

Siena saw the narrow-eyed gaze focused on her and sensed his insouciance was a very thin veneer hiding simmering anger. Futility threatened to overwhelm her. She could try to lie—*again*—make up some excuse. But she did owe this man an explanation. A lot more than an explanation. She owed him his money back.

Carefully she put down her drink. Her mind was whirling

with what she was contemplating. Could she just...*tell* him? Appeal to his sense of compassion? After all, hadn't she seen it in action?

Knowing that her sister was finally safe and would be looked after for the forseeable future, and telling herself that she didn't have to divulge *everything,* Siena tried to glean some encouragement from Andreas's expressionless face.

She looked down at her hands in her lap for a long moment, and just before the silence stretched to breaking point said quietly, 'The money was for my sister, not me.'

Silence met her words, and she looked up to see Andreas was genuinely confused. 'You said she was in the South of France with friends...'

Siena could see when understanding dawned, but it was the wrong kind of understanding, and she winced when he spoke.

'*She* needed the money? To fund her debauched lifestyle? *That's* why you were willing to prostitute yourself?'

His crude words drove Siena up out of the chair. She realised somewhat belatedly that she would never have got away with such a flimsy explanation. Her whole body was taut, quivering.

'No. It's not like that.' Siena bit her lip and took a terrifying leap of faith. 'Serena was never in the South of France. She's here. In England. She came with me when we left Italy. I lied.'

Andreas's mouth twisted, 'I know your proficiency for lies, Siena. Tell me something I don't know.'

Siena winced again, but she knew she deserved it. Unable to bear being under Andreas's scrutiny like this, she moved jerkily over to the other window and crossed her arms, staring out at the view as if it would magically transport her out of this room.

'My sister...is ill. She's had mental health issues for years. They probably started not long after our mother died, I was three and Serena was five. She had always been a difficult child…I remember tantrums and our father locking her in her room. Her illness manifested itself as bouts of severe depression in her early teens, along with more manic periods when she would go out and go crazy. It got so bad that she had psychotic episodes and hallucinations. She tried to take her own life during one of those times…not to mention developing a drink and drug addiction.'

Siena heard nothing from Andreas, and was too scared to look at him, so she continued, 'Our father was disgusted at this frailty and refused to deal with it. It was only after her suicide attempt that she was diagnosed with severe bipolar disorder. Our father wouldn't allow her to take medication for fear that it would leak to the press…' Siena's voice grew bitter. 'Despite her party girl reputation she was still a valuable heiress—albeit slightly less valuable than me.'

Siena closed her eyes briefly, praying for strength in the face of Andreas's scorn, and turned to face him. His face was still expressionless.

'Go on,' he said coolly.

'When our father disappeared Serena went through a manic phase. It was impossible to control her. Physically she's stronger than me, and her drinking was out of control. All I could do was wait until the inevitable fall and then persuade her to come to England. She knew she needed help. She wanted help. I found a good psychiatric clinic and she was accepted. I had some money left over from our mother's inheritance that hadn't been seized by the authorities and that paid for our move, and for Serena for the first few months of her treatment. It's complicated, because she has to be treated for her addictions first.'

Siena looked away, embarrassed by her own miscalculation. 'I thought that with my wages I could continue to pay for her upkeep, but I hadn't really factored in the weekly cost. When I met you…again…there was only enough money left for a few weeks. She's at a delicate stage in her treatment. If she'd had to leave now because we couldn't afford it, the doctors warned me that it could be catastrophic.'

Siena braced herself for Andreas's reaction, remembering all too well their father's archaic views on mental illness.

Desperate to try and defend her sister, Siena looked back, eyes blazing. 'She's not just some vacuous socialite. It *is* a disease. If you could have seen her…the pain and anguish… and there was nothing I could do…'

To Siena's chagrin, hot tears prickled and she quickly blinked them back. 'She's my sister, and I'll do anything to try and help her. She's all I have left in the world.'

'What about your half-brother?' Andreas asked quietly.

Siena still couldn't make out his expression and her heart constricted when she thought of Rocco.

'I knew I could never go to him. You saw yourself what his reaction was. I expected it. I remember that day he spoke of. It's etched into my memory.' Quietly she said, 'I didn't mean what I said about him…afterwards. I was angry and felt vulnerable. The day we saw him confront our father, if Serena or I had so much as looked in his direction we would have been punished mercilessly. You have no idea what our father was capable of.'

'Why don't you tell me?'

Siena felt as if she was in some kind of a dreamlike state. Andreas was asking these innocuous questions that cut to the very heart of her, making her talk about things that she'd talked about with no one. *Ever.* Not even Serena.

Her legs suddenly felt weak and she went back to the couch and sat down. She looked up at Andreas and said starkly, 'He was a sadist. He took pleasure from other people's pain. But especially Serena, because she had always been so wilful and difficult to control. She became his punching bag because he knew that I was the one he could depend on to perform, to be good.'

Siena took a shaky breath and glanced at her pale hands. 'I learnt what would happen from an early age if I wasn't good. He caught me painting over one of the *palazzo* murals one day...a painter had left some paints behind. He told me to follow him and sent for Serena. He brought us into his study and told Serena to hold out her hand. He took a bamboo stick out of his cupboard and whipped her until she was bleeding. Then he told me that if I ever misbehaved again this was what would happen: Serena would be punished.'

Siena looked at Andreas. She felt cold inside. 'Serena didn't blame me. Not then. *Never.* It was as if in spite of her own turmoil she knew that what he was doing was just as damaging to me.'

Andreas's voice was impossibly grim, sending a shiver down Siena's spine. 'How old were you when this happened?'

'Five.'

For long seconds there was silence. Siena fancied she could see something in Andreas's eyes. His jaw twitched, and then he said, 'I want you to tell me what happened in Paris that night.'

Siena had known it would come to this. She owed Andreas this much. An explanation. Finally. Not that it could change the past or absolve her of her sins.

She fought to remain impassive, not to appear as if this was shredding her insides to bits. 'That evening in Paris... when my father caught us...I panicked. I had not premeditated what happened. I was overwhelmed at the strength of the attraction between us. I'd noticed you all evening. I'd never felt anything like it before...'

Siena looked back at her hands. 'I know you might not believe that...especially after I tried to make you believe I was more experienced than I was...' She was afraid of what she'd see if she looked at him so she kept her gaze down. 'When my father appeared I knew instantly what I had done—how bad it was. Serena was going through a rough patch. She was at home in Florence, being supervised by a doctor, but only because I had begged our father not to leave her alone...I was terrified of what he would do if he thought that what we'd been doing had been...mutual.'

Siena felt movement and then Andreas was sitting down beside her. His fingers were on her chin and he was forcing her to look at him. Her belly somersaulted at the look in his eyes. It was burning.

'You're telling me that you *didn't* set out to seduce me? That it *wasn't* just boredom? And that you only denounced me out of fear of what your father would do?'

Siena swallowed. Shame filled her belly. She whispered, 'Yes. I was a coward. I chose to protect my own sister over you... But I had no idea how far my father would go.'

Andreas let her chin go and stood up, his whole body vibrating with tension—or anger. Siena couldn't make out which.

And then he exploded, '*Theos,* Siena. You wilfully ruined my life just because you were too scared to stand up to your *father?*'

Siena stood up. It was as if a lead weight was making her belly plummet. She should have expected this, but still her head swam and her stomach churned. 'I'm sorry, Andreas... so sorry. I went looking for you that night to try and explain...'

Suddenly Siena's powers of speech failed her. All she could see was Andreas's eyes, burning into her, scorching her. With a soft cry she felt the world fall away, and only heard the faintest of guttural curses before everything went black.

CHAPTER NINE

ANDREAS STOOD WATCHING Siena's sleeping form on the bed. He'd only just managed to catch her before she crumpled to the floor, and he cursed himself for lashing out. Emotions had roiled in his gut. He'd been so angry—incandescent—to learn the truth of what had happened. *If it was the truth.*

A small part of him wanted to insist that she was lying—making it up, thinking on her feet—but he'd seen the ashy pallor of her face. The way her eyes had looked inward, not even seeing him. No one could have faked that.

The magnitude of what this meant, how it changed things, was impossible to take in. *If it was the truth.*

Andreas threw off his jacket and dropped it to a nearby chair, where he sat down and pulled at his bow-tie. He'd taken off Siena's shoes and covered her with a blanket. From here he could see that perfect profile, the shape of her body, and he felt the inevitable beat of desire. It had surged into his blood as soon as he'd seen her again, as if it had merely lain dormant.

His fists clenched. The thing was, could he believe her? Andreas's mind went back to that cataclysmic evening, and when he thought about it now, without the haze of anger and rage, he could remember that Siena had been icy, yes, but there had been something else in her eyes. Terror?

Her father had had a tight grip on her arm. Too tight. He'd

forgotten that detail. And her father had fed her the words: *'You would never kiss someone like him, would you?'*

Andreas felt disgust. She'd been a day away from eighteen. Innocent. Naïve. Terrified of her father. And not for herself, for her vulnerable sister.

Questions piled on top of questions.

Andreas frowned as another wisp of a memory returned. He'd been called to his boss's office after DePiero's henchmen had laid into him, and had had to explain what had happened.

Andreas had been so angry at his own pathetic naïvety when he should have known better that he'd lashed out. Tried to make it seem, at least to himself, as if he might have had some control over the situation. At one point they'd heard a noise outside and Andreas had gone to the door, which had been ajar. He'd looked out and thought he was seeing things when a flash of ballgown disappeared around a corner.

Had that been Siena? Looking for him? Andreas frowned deeper, trying to remember what he'd said, and it came back in all its brutal clarity: *'I'd never have touched her if I'd known she was so poisonous...'*

He could laugh now. As if he'd had a choice! As if he'd have been able to stop himself from touching her! She'd enthralled him then and she enthralled him today. He was incapable of not touching her if she was within feet of him.

Uneasiness prickled over Andreas's skin. Without the anger and rage he'd clung onto for so long he felt stripped bare and made raw by all these revelations. And yet one thing was immutable: now that Siena was back in his life he was not about to let her go again easily.

When Siena woke she was completely disorientated. She had no idea who or where she was. And then details started emerging. She was in a huge bed and what looked like a misty dawn light was coming through the open curtains. She could see only sky.

She looked around and saw a palatial room, rococo design. She frowned. How did she know it was rococo? She was covered in a soft blanket and her head felt sore. Siena raised it and winced when her hair tugged. She pulled it free of the band, loosening it.

She pulled back the blanket and saw she was in a white shirt and black skirt. It all came rushing back. The reception. *Seeing Andreas.* Him pulling her out, bringing her here. All her words tumbling out. She'd told him...*everything.* He'd been angry. And she'd fainted. Siena was disgusted with herself.

Siena put a hand over her eyes, as if that could stop the painful recollections. Slowly she sat up and pushed the blanket aside, stumbled on jelly legs to the bathroom. When she saw herself in the mirror she made a face. She looked wan and washed out, her hair all over the place. She felt sticky in her uniform. She saw the shower and longed to feel clean again, so she stripped off and turned on the powerful spray, stepped under the teeming water.

Andreas. She shivered. After washing herself thoroughly Siena stepped out and dried herself off. It was time to face Andreas in the cold light of day.

When Siena emerged into the main reception room of the sumptuous suite she still wasn't prepared to see Andreas sitting at a table, drinking coffee and eating some breakfast. She'd dressed in her shirt and skirt, leaving off the bow-tie and shoes. She was barefoot and felt self-conscious now—which was ridiculous when this man knew every inch of her body in intimate detail.

Andreas lowered his paper and stood up. A chivalrous gesture that caught at Siena somewhere vulnerable. She moved forward, her heart thumping against her breastbone. 'I'm sorry.' Her voice was husky. 'I don't know what came over me... Thank you for letting me sleep.'

Andreas pulled out a chair at right angles to his and said coolly, 'Sit down and have something to eat. You've lost weight.'

Siena came forward and avoided his eye. She *had* lost weight. She'd hadn't had much money for food. Sensing his gaze, Siena looked at Andreas and it was intense.

Tightly he said, 'I'm sorry for lashing out at you like that last night... It was just...a lot to take in.'

Siena's heart contracted. 'I know. I'm sorry.'

'I checked out what you told me about Serena.' He sounded defensive. 'I would have been a fool not to after everything...'

The brief warmth that had invaded Siena cooled. 'Of course.'

Siena felt fear trickle down her spine even as hurt lanced her. He hadn't trusted her. 'What are you going to do?'

Andreas's mouth tightened. 'Nothing. Your sister deserves all the care she can get after a lifetime of being subjected to that kind of treatment.'

Siena felt momentarily dizzy. 'Thank you,' she said, and then she blurted out, 'I'll pay you back...the money. If you could let me set up a payment plan...?'

Andreas looked at her incredulously. 'On the kind of wages you've been earning? You'd be paying me out of your pension.'

Siena flushed and straightened her back, clinging to the small amount of pride she had left. 'I'll find another job. There are grants for people on minimum wage, training schemes...'

Andreas was grim. He poured her some coffee and pushed a plate of bread towards her. 'You don't need to pay me back. If you'd told me in the first place what you needed the money for I would have helped you.'

Now Siena was the one to look at him incredulously, and she remarked bitterly, 'Forgive me if I don't believe you. You hate my guts. You wanted revenge. If I had told you that my feckless sister was in a clinic to sort out her addictions and mental health issues you would have sneered in my face.' Siena looked down. 'I was afraid you might try to use her to get back at me—after all, that's what my father always did.'

Siena missed the way Andreas winced slightly.

He said heavily, 'My best friend committed suicide years ago, and I witnessed the devastation it wrought. I don't underestimate mental health illness for a second. I might not have been initially inclined to help, but if you had explained to me—'

Siena looked up, unsettled by this nugget from his past. 'What? Explained the tawdry reality of our lives? The sadistic bullying of our father?'

Andreas's eyes narrowed on her. 'Why did Serena not leave once she could?'

Siena swallowed, 'She didn't leave because of me. She wouldn't leave me behind. And then…once I got older…she was too dependent on our father's money to fuel her drink and drugs addiction. When she *could* have left she didn't want to. As perverse as that sounds.'

Andreas was grim. 'And so as long as she stayed you were stuck too?'

Siena nodded.

Andreas put down his napkin. 'Now that I know…everything…I will take care of Serena's bills. You don't have to pay me back.'

Siena's heart lurched. 'But I do. You don't owe me—*us*—anything.' The line of her mouth was bitter. 'I owe you so much. More than I can ever repay. If it wasn't for me you would never have been sacked or had to leave Europe.'

To Siena's dismay she could feel tears threaten, but she forced herself to look at Andreas. 'You don't know how much I wanted to go back in time, to undo what happened.'

Andreas's eyes grew darker and he leaned forward. 'That's wishful thinking. If we had that moment over again nothing could have kept us from touching each other. It was inevitable.'

Siena's heart beat faster. Her belly swooped. 'What are you saying?'

'What I'm saying is that the chemistry between us was too powerful to ignore. Then and now.'

Stupidly Siena repeated, *'Now?'*

Andreas nodded and stood up. He came around the table and took Siena's hands, pulling her up out of her chair. He was suddenly very close, very tall. Siena could feel his heat reach out and envelop her, and a wave of intense longing came over her, setting her whole body alight. She'd not even admitted to herself how much she'd missed him in the past month, how she'd ached for him at night.

'We're not done, Siena.'

Andreas put his hand to the back of her neck, fingers tangling in her hair, and urged her closer. And then his mouth was on hers, hot and urgent. She could feel him hardening against her belly and she groaned. She couldn't deny this either—not when every cell in her body was rejoicing.

She lifted her arms and fisted her hands in Andreas's hair, bolder than she'd been before, arching herself into him. The knowledge resounded in her head. He knew everything but he still wanted her. She'd believed his desire had died a death the night he'd let her go. A fierce exultation made her blood surge, and her heart soared when he pulled back and looked at her for an incendiary moment. She felt him picking her up and quickly covering the distance back to the bedroom.

As he was lying her on the bed Andreas was already opening the buttons of her shirt, and Siena's hands were mirroring his. She almost wept when her fingers were too clumsy. Andreas took her hands away and ripped it open, buttons popping everywhere.

An urgency that Siena hadn't experienced before infused the air around them. Her shirt was open and Andreas pulled the cups of her bra down so that her breasts spilled free. He bent his head to pay homage to the puckered peaks, making Siena cry out at the exquisite sensation.

Siena barely noticed that Andreas was arching her into him so that he could undo her skirt at the back, but then his mouth was gone and he was lying her down again so that he could pull her skirt over her hips and thighs and off.

It was hard to breathe. Especially when she saw his hands go to his belt and he made quick work of taking off his trousers and boxers. And then he was naked. And aroused. Siena's heart-rate increased when she saw the telltale moisture bead at the tip of his erection, and a gush of heat made her even wetter between her legs.

Andreas came down on the bed beside her, the rising sun outside making his body gleam. With deft hands her shirt and bra followed her clothes and his to the floor and soon they were both naked.

A surge of something scarily tender gripped Siena. She raised a hand and touched Andreas's jaw, relishing the stubble prickling against her palm.

He took her hand and brought it down, curling her fingers around him. Her eyes widened when she felt the solid strength of him, how he twitched and seemed to swell even more. Her hand moved up and down in an instinctive rhythm and Siena watched Andreas's cheeks flush with blood, his eyes grow even darker.

Stretching up, she pressed her mouth to his, open, her tongue seeking and finding his, sucking it deep. Her breasts were full and tight, and Andreas's hand moved down her body until he pushed between her legs, making them fall apart. His fingers found the moist evidence of her arousal and stroked with a rhythm that made her curve into him, pull her mouth from his so she could suck in oxygen.

And then his fingers thrust into her, and Siena's body spasmed with pre-orgasmic pleasure.

Andreas's voice was guttural, rough. 'You're so ready for me. I want you *now*. I've missed you.'

'I've missed you.' Siena's heart stopped for a long second and she searched Andreas's face. He looked as if he was in a fever. She slammed down on the momentary joy his words had provoked. He was talking in the heat of the moment, that was all.

Her whole body seemed to be poised on the brink. She felt Andreas take her hand from him and heard the ripping of foil, and then he was back, the blunt head of his erection pressing against her body, teasing.

Siena opened her legs wider, bit her lip and arched upwards, forcing Andreas to impale her. The pleasure was like nothing she'd experienced yet with this man. It was more intense than anything before.

Andreas slid deep into her body before pulling out again, and then moved back in. Siena's head went back and she looked up at him, her chest feeling so full that she could only gasp when he slid so deep that it felt as if he touched her heart…and in that moment the knowledge burst into Siena's consciousness.

She loved this man. She loved him as she'd never loved another being—not even her sister.

But she couldn't fully absorb it. Andreas was wresting away her ability to think as his powerful body surged, robbing her of breath and speech.

The intense dance between their bodies became all she could focus on. She was willing herself not to tip over the edge too soon, revelling in Andreas's power and control. But then it became too much. She couldn't hang on. Not when she wrapped her legs around Andreas's hips and their chests were crushed together. And not when he bent his head and found one taut peak, sucked it deep.

Siena cried out as emotion soared and realisation struck her: she'd thought she'd never experience this again.

Her body tightened on that delicious plateau just a second before she fell and fell, her body clenching tight around Andreas's shaft, urging him on until he too fell and their bodies were just a sweaty tangle of limbs on the tousled covers of the bed.

When Siena woke again she was disorientated once more, but this time because Andreas was in bed with her, his head resting on one hand as he looked at her. She blushed, and he smiled, and her heart palpitated. So much had happened in the space of twenty-four hours.

His smile faded. 'I want you to come home with me.'

Those words caused a lurch in Siena's chest. 'Home? To your apartment?'

Andreas nodded, and then said with familiar intractability, 'I'm not going to take no for an answer. You're coming with me, Siena.'

She looked at him for a long moment. His jaw was more stubbled now. He had that look she recognized. Slightly stern. Determined.

Feeling claustrophobic under his dark blue gaze, Siena looked away and saw the bathroom robe at the end of the bed, where she'd thrown it earlier. Moving before she could lose her nerve, she sat up and reached for it, pulling it around her and awkwardly feeding her arms into the sleeves. She got out of the bed to stand apart from him, belting the robe tightly and trying not to think of how dishevelled she felt. *How deliciously sated.*

'Andreas...' she began, not really knowing what to say.

He lay back against the pillows, arms behind his head, broad chest swelling with the movement, and Siena was hopelessly distracted for a moment.

With an effort she tore her avid gaze away and looked back to his eyes, narrowed on her. She started again. 'Andreas.'

He arched a brow.

'Things are...different now. I owe you a huge sum of money.' Siena blushed. 'I didn't feel comfortable taking the jewellery, or cashing it in, but I felt as if taking care of Serena was more important than my guilty conscience.'

She steeled herself, but it was hard when Andreas was like a lounging pasha in the bed.

'But now I won't feel comfortable unless you let me come to some agreement. I can't. It's not right. Not with everything else that has happened. I'd prefer to let you have your money back and try to take care of Serena myself than let you pay.'

Andreas sat up. 'That is not an option. Not now that I know what her situation is. You *will* let me pay, Siena.'

Siena wrung her hands and all but wailed. 'But can't you see? I'll be beholden to you for ever. I can't have that. My father was a tyrant...he owned us.' She saw a dangerous look on Andreas's face but rushed on. 'I'm not saying you're the same...but I couldn't bear to go back into that kind of...obligation.'

Andreas rested his arms on his knees, still managing to look intimidating despite his being naked under the sheets.

'You weren't so conflicted when you walked away with a fortune in jewellery.'

Siena's face grew hotter. 'I didn't think I'd ever see you again. I only took it because I thought I was making the best choice—that the end justified the means.' She hitched her chin. 'You were only too happy to let me walk away. And it's not as if you got nothing in return.'

His eyes flashed, but he said silkily, 'That's true. After all

I got the precious DePiero innocence. But now I want you to come back to me.'

'Come back to me.' Siena felt weak. Questions reverberated in her head: *For how long? Why? Is it just about the sex?*

A voice answered her. *Of course it was just about the sex.*

'I—' Siena began, but Andreas cut in harshly.

'We both know I can have you flat on your back moaning with need in seconds—don't think I won't prove to you that you can't just walk away from this.'

Andreas didn't like the feeling of panic that gripped him when her eyes grew wide. He had nothing to hold Siena now. Not really. Only a complete lowlife would make her pay him back for her sister's treatment.

So quietly that he almost didn't hear her, Siena said, 'If I come back to you I want things to be different.'

Andreas went still, not liking the way his blood surged. She looked serious, and heart-stoppingly beautiful with her hair feathered over her shoulders.

'I want to find a job—a better job if I can—and start paying you back.' Andreas opened his mouth but Siena held up a hand, stopping him. 'That's non-negotiable. I have some skills…I can type and file. I used to act as my father's secretary when his PA was off or on leave, and I worked sometimes at a local school, helping the special needs assistants. I'm hoping that will count for something.'

'Also, I don't want any more jewellery.' She shuddered slightly. 'I don't want to see another piece of jewellery as long as I live.'

'Anything else?' Andreas prompted, seeing her biting her lip and feeling the rush of need make him harden again.

'As soon as this…chemistry…whatever it is…is over it ends. Because it won't last for ever, will it? It can't…'

There was a tinge of desperation to her voice that resonated in Andreas and he held out a hand. 'It's not over yet... Come here, Siena.'

She stood stubbornly apart. 'Do you agree? To what I've said?'

'Yes,' Andreas growled, his need making his voice sound harsh. 'Now come here.'

Six weeks later.

''Night, Siena. See you on Monday. Have a good weekend.'

Siena smiled. ''Night, Lucy. I hope your little girl feels better soon.'

The other woman left and the door swung shut behind her. Siena looked around and stretched. She was the only one left in the typing pool. She was due to receive her very first paycheck next week, and it was almost embarrassing how excited she was about it.

Sometimes she couldn't fathom how lucky she was: Serena was safe and secure, and receiving the best treatment, and Siena was fulfilling a lifelong ambition to be independent. Well, she qualified, as independent as she could be with a dominant alpha male lover who resented everything that took her away from him. Even though, as she'd pointed out heatedly, he didn't count *his* work in that equation...

She got up and went to the rack to get her coat. She looked out of the window. A spurt of desire heated her insides when she saw a familiar silver sports car and Andreas standing beside it, phone to his ear.

She hadn't seen him in two days as he'd been in New York on business.

She'd been working here for almost a month now, but he insisted on picking her up every day, or having his driver do it.

He'd grumbled in bed the other morning at dawn, 'I want

you to come with me. *Why* do you insist on working when you don't have to?'

Siena had rolled her eyes. It was a familiar argument, but she stuck to her guns, not wanting to lay out in bald language that one day, when Andreas stopped desiring her, she'd be on her own again.

He was the one who had patiently helped her put together a CV which flagrantly glossed over the fact that she had no *bona fide* qualifications. He'd pulled her close on his lap and they'd sat in his study in front of his computer. 'Anyway, it doesn't matter," he'd said. "You'll walk into the office and they'll all be drooling too hard to even notice what's on your CV...'

Siena had punched him playfully, hating the see-saw emotions that still gripped her in his presence. It was different this time. *He* was different. Not more open, exactly—he always kept a piece of himself back—but she was seeing a side to him now that made her fall for him a little more each day. He was lighter, made her laugh.

It reminded her painfully of what it had been like the evening they'd met in Paris, before the world had crashed down around them. She resolutely pushed aside the painful knowledge that for him it had just been an opportunity...

When she'd got the job, after two rounds of interviews, Andreas had surprised her by cooking a traditional Greek dinner and producing a bottle of champagne with a flourish.

Siena could see him now, looking at the door of her building with barely disguised impatience, and hurriedly put on her coat and got her bag. As she went downstairs she reflected that Andreas still hadn't ever really opened up to her about his personal life. After mentioning his family the last time, and the way he'd shut down, she didn't like to bring it up.

After all, she thought a little bleakly, what was the point? It wasn't as if she was ever likely to become a more permanent fixture in Andreas's life.

When she got outside the breath stuck in her throat at the narrow-eyed, heavy-lidded look he gave her. She wasn't unaware of the interest of women passing by, and a fierce surge of possessiveness gripped her. A primal reaction of a woman to her mate.

He put his phone in his pocket and caught her to him, slanting his mouth across hers in a kiss that was not designed for public consumption. Siena didn't care, though. Two days felt like two months, and she arched her body into his and fisted her hands in his hair.

When he pulled away he chuckled and said, 'Miss me, then?'

Siena blushed. She was so *raw* around him. She affected an airy look and said, 'Not at all. How long were you gone anyway?'

The ease that had built up between them in the past few weeks made Siena feel dizzy sometimes. It was so different from how it had been before.

Andreas scowled. 'You'll pay for that. *Later.*'

He stepped back and opened the car door, letting Siena get in. She took a deep breath, watching him walk around the car with that powerful, leonine grace, and her belly somersaulted.

When he got in she felt unaccountably shy. 'My boss came and told me today that I might be getting a promotion—moving up to work with someone as a personal secretary within another month.'

Andreas looked at her and put a large hand on her leg, under her skirt, inched it up. 'I can offer you a promotion if you want—to my bed.'

Siena rolled her eyes and stopped Andreas's hand with her own—mostly because she was embarrassed by how turned on she already was.

'I'm already in your bed. You know I'm not going to give up my job...'

Andreas rolled his eyes and put his hand back on the wheel. 'At least they won't be demanding your attention over the weekend. You're mine for the next forty-eight hours, DePiero.'

Siena noticed then that they weren't taking the turn for where he lived in Mayfair and asked idly, 'Where are we going?'

Andreas glanced at her and looked a little sheepish.

Instantly Siena's eyes narrowed. 'Andreas Xenakis, what are you up to?'

He sighed. 'We're going to Athens for the weekend.' As if he could see her start to protest he held up a hand and said, 'I promise you'll be back at your desk by nine on Monday morning.'

'But I don't have anything with me—do you have to go to a function?'

Andreas nodded. 'It's a charity ball. I instructed my secretary to go to the apartment and pack some clothes, get your passport.'

At times like this it still stunned Siena how much power Andreas had.

They hadn't been to many functions in the last few weeks, but then Andreas said, with an edge to his voice, 'My youngest sister has just had a new baby. I promised my parents we'd call for lunch on Sunday before going home.'

Siena tamped down the flutters in her belly when he said *'we'*. 'Oh?' she said, in a carefully neutral voice. 'That sounds nice.'

She avoided Andreas's eyes, not wanting him to remember how he'd reacted when she'd asked him about his family before. Not wanting to remind him of *before* at all.

The following evening, in the ballroom of the hotel where they were staying, Andreas looked at Siena weaving through the crowd as she came back from the ladies' room. The ache that seemed to have set up residence in his gut intensified. She was wearing the black dress she'd worn on their first night out—except this time her face wasn't a mask of faint hauteur and she wore only the gold birdcage necklace.

It was so obvious now that she'd put on a monumental act when she'd been with him for that week. Uncomfortably he had to concede the many signs had given her away, if he'd cared to investigate them at the time. Her antipathy for the jewellery, her visible reluctance at being on the social scene, which he'd put down to embarrassment but which he now knew went deeper. *Her innocence.* Both physically and actually.

When Andreas thought of her father, he wanted to throttle the man.

And even though her brother was a billionaire she hadn't attempted to go to him for a hand-out.

Siena's make-up was as subtle as ever, and yet she outshone every woman in the room. She *glowed.* She saw him in the crowd and she smiled—a small, private smile. Andreas wanted to smile back—he could feel the warmth rising up within him, something deeper than mere lust and desire—but something held him back. That ache inside him was unyielding.

He saw Siena's smile falter slightly and fade. Her eyes dropped and Andreas felt inexplicably as if he was losing something. Someone waving caught his eye and he looked over to see a familiar face with relief. He welcomed the distraction from thinking too much about the way Siena made him feel.

When she arrived by his side, however, he couldn't stop himself from snaking an arm around her, relishing her proximity. *His.* It beat like a tattoo in his blood.

Belying his turbulent emotions, he said, 'How would you like to meet the designer of your necklace? She's the wife of a friend of mine and they're just across the room.'

Siena's hand flew to the gold chain and she looked up, eyes

wide and bright. 'Really? Angel Parnassus is here? I'd *love* to meet her!'

As Andreas led Siena by the hand through the crowd he pushed down the way her simple joy at meeting a mere jewellery designer made something inside him weaken. Things might have changed but the essentials were the same. Siena was with him only until he could let her go…and that day would come. *Soon.*

CHAPTER TEN

ANDREAS HAD ORGANISED a helicopter to take them from Athens on Sunday to a small landing pad near his parents' town. Siena couldn't stop the flutters of apprehension in her belly, and wasn't unaware of Andreas's almost tangible tension.

A four-wheel drive vehicle was waiting for them at the landing pad and soon they were driving out and ascending what looked like a mountain.

Curiously, Siena asked, 'How often do you come home?'

Andreas's profile was remote. 'Not often enough for my mother.'

Siena smiled but Andreas didn't. She couldn't understand his reluctance to come home. If she'd come from a family like his she didn't think she'd ever have left...

She could see a town now, colourful and perched precariously on a hill above them. 'Is that it?'

'Yes,' Andreas answered.

When they drove in Siena looked around with interest. It looked modestly prosperous—wide clean streets, people walking around browsing market stalls and colourful shops. They looked friendly and happy. Siena could see a lot of construction work going on and had an instinct that Andreas was involved, for all his apparent reluctance to come home.

They drove up through winding streets until they emerged

into a beautifully picturesque square with a medieval church and very old trees.

Andreas came to a stop and Siena opened her seat belt, saying, 'This is beautiful.'

'You can see all the way to Athens on a clear day.'

'I can believe that,' Siena breathed, taking in the stunning view.

Andreas got out and she followed suit, and suddenly from around the corner came a screaming gaggle of children. They swarmed all over Andreas, and Siena's heart twisted at seeing him lift a little one high in the air with a huge smile on his face.

She intuited that he might not like coming home, for whatever reason, but he loved his family.

He put the child down and the other children disappeared as quickly as they'd arrived. He held out his hand for her and smiled wryly. 'Some of my nieces and nephews. They'll have heard the helicopter.'

Siena took his hand. She'd followed his lead, dressing down in smart jeans and a soft dusky pink silk top with a light grey cardigan. Flat shoes made her feel even smaller next to Andreas, fragile, and it wasn't altogether welcome.

As they approached a very modest-looking stone house, with trailing flowers around the windows and door, there were shouts and laughter coming from inside and a baby's wail. Siena unconsciously gripped Andreas's hand, making him look at her.

'Okay?'

She smiled and gulped. 'Yes. Fine.' But she wasn't. Because she'd suddenly realised that if Andreas's family were as idyllic as she feared they might be it would break her open.

But it was too late to turn back. A small, rotund grey-haired woman had come bustling out and was drawing Andreas down to kiss him loudly on the cheeks. When he straightened she had tears in her eyes and was saying, 'My boy...my boy...'

Then Andreas drew Siena forward and introduced her in Greek, of which Siena could only understand a little. His mother looked her up and down and then took her by the arms in a surprisingly strong grip. She nodded once, as if Siena had passed some test, and drew her into her huge soft bosom, kissing her soundly.

Siena felt inexplicably shy and blushed profusely, not used to this amount of touching from a stranger. But Andreas's mother had her hand in hers and was leading her into a lovely bright house, very simple.

There seemed to be a bewildering amount of people and Siena tried to remember all of Andreas's sisters' names: Arachne, who had the new baby, which slept peacefully in a corner; Martha, Eleni, Phebe and Ianthe. They were all dark and very pretty, with flashing eyes and big smiles.

Andreas brought Siena over to meet his father, whom she could see was quite bowed with arthritis, but it was easy to see where Andreas's tall good looks had come from. The man was innately proud, his face marked with the strong lines of his forebears.

Lunch was a somewhat chaotic affair, with children running in and out and everyone talking over everyone else. But the love and affection was palpable. Andreas had one of his nephews curled up trustingly in his lap, and Siena's womb clenched as she saw how at ease he was with the children.

And then Siena recalled his cruel words when she had asked him if he wanted children.

When Arachne, his youngest sister, approached Siena after lunch with the new baby Siena froze with panic. Being faced with this brought up all her deepest longings and fears. For how could she ever be a mother when she had no idea what it felt like to *have* a mother?

But Arachne wouldn't take no for an answer and she handed the baby into Siena's arms, showing her how to hold her.

Andreas had seen Siena's look of horror when Arachne approached her with the baby and had got up, incensed at the thought that she was rejecting his family, but his mother stopped him.

'Wait. Let her be,' she said.

It was only then that Andreas watched and saw Siena's look of horror replaced by one of intense awe and wonder. He realised it hadn't been horror. It had been panic. He could remember his own panic when he'd held a baby for the first time. He realised that Siena had never held a baby before.

Before he could stop himself he was walking over to sit beside her.

She glanced at him and smiled tremulously. 'She's so perfect and tiny. I'm afraid I'll hurt her.'

'You won't,' Andreas said through the tightness in his throat. To see the baby at Siena's breast, Siena's hair falling down over her cheek, her little finger clutched in a tiny chubby hand... Andreas dreaded the inevitable rise of claustrophobia but it didn't come. Something else came in its place—a welling of emotion that he couldn't understand and which wasn't the habitual grief for his dead best friend that he usually felt in this place. This felt new. Far more fragile. Tender. *Dangerous*.

When the baby mewled Siena tensed and whispered, 'What did I do?'

Weakly, Andreas used it as an excuse to break up that disturbing image, gently taking his niece and putting her over his shoulder, patting her back like a professional. Siena's worried face made emotion swell.

'Nothing,' he said gruffly. 'She's probably just hungry again.'

His sister came and took the baby out of Andreas's hands. Andreas watched as Siena stared after Arachne and the baby with an almost wistful look on her face. That galvanised him into moving up onto his feet and he caught her by the hand. She looked at him.

'We should leave if we're to get back to Athens and make our flight slot this evening.'

Just then Andreas's mother came up. She was saying something but she was speaking too fast for Siena to understand. When she was finished Siena asked, 'What did she say?'

Andreas looked at Siena with an unreadable expression. 'She asked if we'd stay for the night…'

Siena couldn't help the silly fluttering of something, but then Andreas reminded her, 'You have to be back for work in the morning.'

Siena's stomach fell. *Work*. 'Oh, yes…'

Andreas's eyes glinted. 'You don't want to miss that, do you?'

Siena looked at him and saw the challenge. He would stay if she relented over her work. She met it head-on and took her hand out of his. 'No, I don't.' Even though she found herself wishing that they *could* stay here longer. Not that she would admit it to Andreas.

Andreas's family bade them a friendly farewell, with Andreas suffering under copious kisses and hugs from his sisters and nieces and nephews. And then his mother came and pulled Siena close again, hugging her tight. When she put her away from her his mother tucked some wayward hair behind her ear in an effortless yet profoundly simple maternal gesture.

She looked at Siena with the kindest dark eyes, and Siena felt as if she could see all the way through to her deepest heart's desires and pain. A ball of emotion was spreading inside Siena and for a panicky second she wanted to burst into tears and bury her head in this woman's chest, to seek a kind of comfort she'd only dreamt existed.

But then Andreas was there and the moment was defused. And soon they were back in the Jeep, and in the helicopter, and by the time they'd got to the plane Siena felt as if she was under control again.

'What did you think?'

Siena turned to look at Andreas, where he was sprawled across the other side of the aisle on the small private jet. She'd been avoiding looking at him because she still felt a little raw. How could she begin to explain to this man that seeing his family had been like a dream of hers manifested? All that love and affection in one place...

'I liked them very much.'

'Still,' Andreas said, with something Siena couldn't decipher in his voice, 'it's not really your scene is it? The rustic nature of a backwater like that and a big, sprawling messy family?'

Siena felt nothing for a second, as if protecting herself, and then hurt bloomed—sharp and wounding. After everything he now knew about her Siena couldn't believe that he still had her very much placed in a box.

It seemed as if not much had really changed at all, in spite of the last few weeks. She wanted to berate him, ask him what his issues over going home were, but she was feeling too fragile. Clearly she still had to play a part.

Feeling very brittle, Siena forced a short sharp laugh. 'As you said yourself, we're from worlds apart.'

And she turned her head and looked out of the window, blinking back the hot prickle of tears, feeling like a fool.

Andreas pushed down the uncomfortable awareness that Siena was upset. Bringing her to see his family had been a mistake. He should have gone on his own. Maybe then he wouldn't have seen them in another light, and not in the usual suffocating way he usually did. Maybe then he wouldn't have noticed his father with one of his nieces on his knee, telling her a story. Wouldn't have had to wonder for the first time in his life what the anatomy of his family would have looked like if his father hadn't stayed to support his wife and children.

There were plenty of marriages in that town that were fragmented because the men had had to go to Athens to work, leaving their family behind. But his father had chosen to stay, and as a result they'd all had a very secure and stable upbringing.

Andreas didn't like to acknowledge that seeing Siena in that milieu hadn't been as alien as he'd thought it would be. She'd charmed them all with that effortless grace, and he could recognise now her genuine warmth.

Andreas glanced at Siena but her face was turned away, her hair spilling over her shoulders and touching the curve of her breast. She was not the woman he'd believed her to be. Not in the slightest.

Andreas looked out of the window beside him blindly, as if she might turn her head and see something he struggled to contain. He thought of how quickly she'd dismissed meeting his family and clung to that like a drowning man to a raft. Of course she'd *liked* his family, but she would never be a part of that world in an indelible way.

Andreas assured himself that the very ambiguous emotions she'd evoked when he'd seen her cradle his baby niece had merely been a natural response to his realisation that one day he too would have to settle down and produce an heir. For the first time it wasn't an image that sent a wave of rejection through his body.

But it wouldn't be with Siena DePiero. Never her.

In bed that night, Siena and Andreas came together in a way that Siena could only lament at. This heat was inevitable between them, and it was good at hiding the fact that there was little else. She wished she could be stronger, but she felt as if time was running out and so she seized Andreas between her legs with a fierce grip, urging him on so that when the explosion came it was more intense than it had ever been.

When he was spooning her afterwards, and she was in a half-asleep haze, Siena opened her eyes. What she'd said earlier about Andreas's family hadn't been truthful, and she was sick of lying to him.

She turned so that she was on her back, looking into Andreas's face. He opened slumberous eyes and that heat sizzled between them again. *Already.* Siena ignored it valiantly and put her hand on Andreas's when it started exploring up across her belly.

'No… I wanted to say something to you…'

Siena felt the tension come into Andreas's big body. He removed his hand from her.

She took a deep breath. 'Earlier, when you said that your home town and meeting your family probably wasn't really my scene, I agreed with you… Well, I shouldn't have. Because it's not true. It's more my scene than you could ever know, Andreas. That's the problem. I dreamed my whole life of a family like yours. I longed to know what it would be like to grow up surrounded with love and affection…'

Siena couldn't read Andreas's expression in the dim light but she could imagine she wouldn't like it.

'When your mother hugged me earlier…she really hugged me. I've never felt that before, and it was amazing. I'm glad you took me. It was a privilege to meet them.'

There was a long moment of silence and then Andreas said in a tight voice, 'You should sleep. You have to be up early.'

When Siena's breaths had evened out and he knew she was alseep Andreas carefully took his arms from around her, noting as he did so that not one night since she'd come back had they slept apart. He got out of bed and pulled on a pair of loose sweats and walked out of the bedroom.

He went into the drawing room and spent a long time looking out of the window. Until he could see the faintest smudge of dawn light in the sky. The knowledge resounded inside him that he couldn't keep fighting it.

Then he went into his study and opened his safe and took out a small box. He sat down and opened it and looked at it for a long time. For the first time since he'd met Siena again the dull ache of need and the emotions she caused within him seemed to dissipate.

Eventually he pulled out a drawer and put the box in it, a sense of resolve filling his belly. It was the same sense he'd felt when he'd laid eyes on Siena for the first time in five years, except this time the resolve came with a lot of fear, and not a sense of incipient triumph.

He had to acknowledge, ruefully, that he'd felt many things in the last tumultuous couple of months, and triumph had figured only fleetingly.

A week later

It was Friday evening and Siena was leaving work. Andreas's driver was waiting for her outside the office and she got into the back of the car. Andreas had called earlier to say he'd been held up in Paris, asking if she would come to meet him if he arranged transport. Siena had said yes.

So now she was being taken to his private plane, which would take her to Paris. Trepidation filled her. She wasn't sure what it would be like to be in Paris with Andreas now… He'd been in a strange mood all week. Monosyllabic and yet staring at her intensely if she caught him looking. It made her nervous, and Siena had a very poisonous suspicion that perhaps Andreas wasn't quite done with torturing her. Perhaps he was going to call time on their relationship in Paris, where it had all started?

And yet the other night he'd surprised her by asking her abruptly why she loved the birdcage necklace so much. She'd answered huskily that to her it symbolised freedom. She'd felt silly, and Andreas hadn't mentioned it again.

At night, when they'd made love, it had felt as if there was some added urgency. Siena had felt even more shattered after each time. Last night she'd been aghast to realise she'd been moved to tears, and had quickly got up to go to the bathroom, terrified Andreas would notice...

Siena knew she wouldn't be able to take it for much longer. Being with Andreas was tearing her apart. Perhaps Paris was the place where *she* should end it once and for all if he didn't?

When she got to Paris her heart was heavy and the weather matched her mood: grey and stormy. The hotel was busy, and with a lurch Siena recognised that it must be the weekend of the debutante ball as she saw harassed-looking mothers with spoilt-looking teenagers.

Surely, she thought to herself wildly, Andreas wouldn't be so cruel...

But then he was there, striding towards her, and everything in Siena's world shrank to him. She was in so much trouble. He kissed her, but it was perfunctory, and with a grimace he cast a glance to the young debs and their entourages of stylists and hair and make-up people.

'I'd forgotten the ball was this weekend...'

Relief flooded Siena and she felt a little weak.

Andreas was saying now, 'I've booked dinner. We'll leave in an hour. I just have some things to finish and I'll meet you in the room.'

Siena went up and tried to calm her fractured nerves after seeing the debs and being back here again. *Still* Andreas's mistress. She forced herself to have a relaxing bath, weary after her week in the office but still exultant to be working.

When Andreas arrived he was in a smart black suit, open shirt, and she had dressed in a gold brocade shift dress.

Solicitously Andreas took her arm and led her out to the lift, down to the lobby, and then into his car. He was so silent that Siena asked nervously, 'Penny for them?'

He turned to look at her blankly for a second, a million miles away, and then focused. He smiled tightly. 'Nothing important.'

He looked away again. Siena's sense of foreboding increased.

They were taken to a new restaurant on the top floor of a famous art gallery with grand views over Paris. The Eiffel Tower was so close Siena felt as if they could touch it. They were finishing their meal before Siena realised that they'd had the most innocuous of conversations. Touching on lots, but nothing really. As if they hardly knew each other.

The bill arrived and suddenly Siena felt as if something was slipping out of her grasp. A panicky sensation gripped her, but now Andreas was standing and they were leaving… She took his hand and thought guiltily that if he didn't say anything neither would she.

Andreas didn't make conversation in the car on the way back—again—and Siena was quiet too, not knowing what to say in this weird, heavy silence. When they got back to the hotel one of the duty managers rushed up to Andreas with a worried look.

After a brief, terse conversation Andreas turned to Siena, 'One of the guests at the ball has had a heart attack. I need to make sure everything is being attended to.'

Siena put a hand on his arm. 'I'll come with you if you like?'

Andreas looked at her and his eyes seemed to blaze with something undefinable. But then he said, 'No, you should go to bed. I'll see you in the morning.'

Siena watched him stride away, so tall and proud, master of the domain from where once *she'd* had him cast out. She felt a sense of futility. It would always be between them. Insurmountable.

After Siena had got into bed she tried to stay awake for a long time, in case she heard Andreas return, but sleep claimed her. When she did wake she was groggy, and it felt as if it was still dark outside.

Andreas was saying, 'Siena… I need you to get up… I've laid out some clothes for you.'

Siena sat up woozily and saw Andreas straighten.

'I'll wait for you outside.'

He was dressed in jeans and a light sweater. She saw a pile of clothes on the end of the bed—jeans and a similar sweater for her, and a jacket. He was walking out of the room.

Feeling dazed and confused, wondering if she was dreaming, Siena got up and quickly dressed. She looked outside for a second and saw that it was close to dawn. Where had Andreas been all night?

Pulling her hair back into a knot, she emerged and saw Andreas standing with his back to her in the salon. He turned when she walked in and even now, half-asleep, he took her breath away. His jaw was stubbled.

'Where were you?' she asked huskily.

'Nowhere important. Caught up with the guests. I want to take you somewhere…'

He came and took her by the hand. There was such an intensity to his expression that Siena couldn't decipher it, so she just said, 'Okay.'

When they were in the lift on the way down Andreas looked ahead and didn't say anything. Siena tried to stop her mind from leaping to all sorts of scenarios. She was waking up now, and as they walked through the hushed and quiet lobby she had a painful sense of *déjà-vu*. She thought of another dawn morning, five years ago. Of the turmoil in her heart and head as she'd walked out, unseeing, straight into Andreas's chest.

They walked around the corner of the hotel, intensifying Siena's sense of *déjà-vu,* and then she saw the huge gleaming motorbike. Siena blinked. Maybe she *was* dreaming.

Andreas was letting her hand go and taking out a helmet. When he drew her close to put it on her head Siena knew this was no dream. She couldn't decipher the expression on Andreas's face. It was forbidding. Then he was putting on his own helmet and lifting one leg over to straddle the bike.

He showed her where to put her foot, and with her hand on his shoulder to balance Siena swung her leg over the bike, sliding down into the seat behind Andreas, her front snug against his back.

He lifted up and pushed down and the bike roared to life, shattering the peace of the morning. Andreas reached back and pulled one of Siena's arms around his waist, and then the other one, showing her where to hold him. Her heart was thumping and she knew she was definitely awake as the bike straightened and they took off.

Unbelievably, it was Siena's first time on a motorbike, and she instinctively tightened her arms around Andreas's waist. It was exhilarating—the wind whipping past them, feeling the bike dip dangerously as Andreas took the corners.

When they stopped at a red light he turned his head and said above the noise, 'Okay?'

Siena nodded and then shouted, 'Yes!' when she realised he couldn't see her. And then they were off again.

Siena felt as if they were the only two people in the world as the faintest of pink streaks lined the dawn sky. Only a handful of cars passed them by.

Siena looked at the closed-up shops and bars that only hours before would have been teeming with people. The Eiffel Tower appeared in the distance, grey and stoic in the dawning light, bare of its glittering night-time façade. Siena preferred it like that.

They wound their way through the streets and Siena noticed that they were starting to go uphill. And then she saw the huge white shape of the Sacré Coeur in the distance. Through a series of winding, increasingly narrow streets they got closer and closer, until Andreas brought the bike to a stop under some trees.

He got off and removed his helmet, still with that enigmatic look on his face.

Siena pulled her helmet off and asked, 'Why are we here?'

Andreas took her helmet and said, 'Not yet. Another couple of minutes.'

He put the helmets away and pocketed the keys. He held out his hand. Siena put her hand in his and let him lead her up a path and through a small wooded area until the iconic church loomed above them, stately and awe-inspiring.

They were already quite high up, and Andreas led the way onward until they reached the steps outside the main doors. Siena turned around and saw the whole of Paris laid out in front of them, jaw-dropping in its beauty. She'd seen this view before but never like this, at dawn, without hordes of tourists, and with a dusky mist making everything seem hazy and dreamlike.

There was just one other couple. The woman was wearing what had to be her boyfriend's dinner jacket over a long dress and they were arm in arm, leaning over the balustrade that looked out over the ascent from the hill. They were too engrossed to notice Siena and Andreas.

'Let's sit.'

Siena looked to see Andreas indicate the steps. They sat down. He muttered something that Siena couldn't make out and then said, 'It's too cold.'

The stone *was* cold, but Siena wouldn't have swapped it for the world. 'No, it's fine… Andreas, why are we here?'

For the first time Siena noticed that Andreas was avoiding her eye and then she looked more closely. Her heart lurched. She might almost say that he looked nervous… He seemed to take a deep breath, and then he turned to look at her. The tortured expression on his face nearly took her breath away. Then he took her hands in his and she didn't say anything.

He looked down for a moment, and then back up. Siena had never seen him hesitant like this, and her heart beat fast.

'That morning…the morning after…when you came out of the hotel and I got on my bike and left…this is where I came. I came to this exact spot and sat on these steps and I looked out over this view and I cursed you.' Andreas gripped her hands tight, as if to reassure her, and then he continued.

'But mostly I cursed myself for being so stupid… You see, I thought *I* was the fool, to have been seduced by you. I thought you were like those other debutantes. Worldly-wise and experienced. Spoilt and bored.'

Siena tried to speak, familiar pain gripping her. 'Andreas—'

He shook his head. 'No. Let me speak, okay?'

Siena's heart lurched and she nodded. Andreas looked impossibly young at that moment.

'From the moment I saw you in that room I wanted you. When the opportunity came to be alone with you I jumped at it. And you were nothing like I'd expected. You were sweet and funny, so sexy and innocent.'

His mouth twisted. 'And yet those were all the very things I thought you'd fabricated when you stood at your father's side and denounced me. When his men took me outside I felt I deserved a beating for having been so duped… When I was called into my boss's office I lashed out at you—you received the full brunt of my pain. You see, I was arrogant enough to believe that no woman could enthral me. I wasn't going to have

my head turned so easily. I'd vowed to get out of my small
town and make something of myself. I wasn't going to get
caught up in suffocating domesticity like my father had and
waste my life…and I wasn't going to fall in love with some
girl only to find out she didn't love me, as my friend Spiro did
to his tragic cost. Yet within minutes of setting eyes on you
you'd turned me inside out and I didn't even know it.'

Siena wasn't sure if she was breathing. His eyes burned
like two dark sapphires.

'After what happened I put you down as a rich, cold-hearted
bitch. But I couldn't stop thinking about you. I wanted out of
my world and into your world so badly. I wanted to be able
to stand in front of you some day and show you that I wasn't
nothing. Prove that you had wanted me. You heard that conversation with my boss, didn't you?'

Siena's eyes were locked on Andreas. Slowly she nodded,
and whispered, 'I went looking for you. I wanted to apologise, to explain.'

Andreas's mouth thinned. 'I probably wouldn't have believed you—just like I never gave you the chance to speak
the next morning.'

Siena's hands tightened in his. Her voice was pained. 'You
had to *leave* Europe. *I* did that to you.'

Andreas extricated one hand and lifted it to tuck some
wayward hair behind Siena's ear. He smiled. 'Yes, and it was
probably the best thing that could have happened to me. I got
to America fired up with ambition and anger and energy. I
caught Ruben's eye…and the rest is history. If that night hadn't
happened and I'd stayed here I might be lucky enough to be
managing that hotel now. I certainly wouldn't *own* it… I don't
think I even knew my own potential until I went abroad.'

Siena said fiercely, 'You would have succeeded, no matter what.'

Andreas's hand cupped her jaw and he said seriously,

'Would it even mattter to you if I was just the manager of some middle-of-the-road hotel?'

Siena's heart stopped for a second and then galloped on. She shook her head and said honestly, 'No, not in the slightest.'

Andreas's fingers dropped from her chin and he took her hand again. He looked pained. 'There's something I should have said to you long before now…when you asked me if I wanted children…'

Siena remembered what he'd said that night and started to speak, not wanting to be reminded, but Andreas squeezed her hand.

'No. It was unforgivable and cruel, what I said. You touched a nerve and I lashed out. And I'm sorry. You didn't deserve it. You are not a cold-hearted tease. Any child would be lucky to have you as its mother, Siena.'

Siena felt tears prickle and blinked rapidly. His apology was profound, and she couldn't speak, so she just nodded in acknowledgement. Andreas drew in a shaky breath and reached into the pocket of his jeans to take something out. And then he got down on one knee before her, with the whole of Paris bathed in dawn light behind him.

Her eyes grew huge as she saw that he held a small black velvet box. His hands were shaking.

He looked at her and admitted, 'I can't believe I'm doing this… I always associated this with the death of ambition and success. I had a horror of somehow ending up back in my home town, having nothing. I thought my father had sacrificed too much by not taking up a college scholarship, by getting my mother pregnant and then marrying her having baby after baby. Staying stuck.'

'But your parents…' Siena said softly, still moved by his apology, trying not to let her heart jump out of her chest as she thought about that box. 'They created something wonderful. And if you hadn't had that secure foundation you might never have believed you *could* escape.'

Andreas smiled wryly. 'I know...*now*.' His smile faded slightly. 'When you admitted to me how you felt about meeting my family...my mother...I knew I had to stop fighting it. That I had to stop trying to box you into a place that made it easier for me to deal with you... I tried to make you admit you hated it, but that was only to bolster my own pathetic determination to avoid looking at how it made me feel. The fact is, going home with you...it made all those demons run away. I saw only love and affection. The security. And I felt for the first time as if I could be part of it and not be consumed by it.'

Siena looked from the box to Andreas. He was still on his knees. 'Andreas...?'

He opened the box and Siena looked down to see a beautiful vintage ring nestled in silk folds. It had one large round diamond at its centre, in an Art Deco setting, and was surrounded by small sapphires on either side. It was ornate, but simple, and Siena guessed very old.

Andreas sounded husky. 'I know you said you never wanted another piece of jewelry, but this was my grandmother's engagement ring. My mother gave it to me for my future wife when I was eighteen and heading off to Athens to work for the first time. I resented the implication that I would have to get married. I hated it and everything it symbolised and I vowed that it would be a cold day in hell before I gave it to anyone. Consequently it's languished at the back of many safes over the years—until this week. When I took it out and got it cleaned. Because I'd finally met the one person I could contemplate giving it to.'

Siena felt slightly numbed. Andreas held the ring up now, out of the box, and took her hand. She could feel him trembling—or maybe it was her trembling.

'Siena DePiero...will you do me the honour of becoming

my wife? Because you're in my head and my heart and my soul, and you have been for five years—ever since I first saw you. First you were a fascination, then you became an obsession, and now…I love you. The thought of you being in this world but not with me is more terrifying than anything I've ever known. So, please…will you marry me?'

Siena opened her mouth but all that came out was a sob. Her heart felt as if it was cracking open. Tears blurred her vision. She tried to speak through the vast ball of emotion making her chest full.

'I…' She couldn't do it. She put her hand to her mouth, trying to contain what she felt.

She saw the look on Andreas's face—stark sudden pain as it leached of colour. He thought she was saying *no.* Siena put her trembling hands around Andreas's face and looked at him, fought to contain her emotion just for a moment.

'Yes…Andreas Xenakis…I will marry you.' She drew in a great shuddering breath. 'I love you so much I don't ever want to live without you.'

That was all she could manage before she put her arms around his neck and noisy sobs erupted. His hand was on her back, soothing until the sobs stopped and she could draw back. Siena didn't care how she looked. Andreas was smiling at her as he'd smiled a long time ago, with no shadows of the past between them. Just love.

He took her hand and slid the ring onto her finger. It fitted perfectly and she looked at it in shock, still slightly disbelieving. She looked into his eyes. Her breath hitched. 'That morning…when you left on your bike…I wanted to go with you.'

Andreas smiled and ran his finger down her cheek. 'I wanted to take you with me, even as I cursed you.'

'I wish you had,' Siena whispered, emotional as she thought of the wasted years.

'Your sister,' Andreas reminded her ruefully.

Siena smiled too, a little sadly. 'Yes…my sister.'

Andreas moved back onto the steps beside her and held her face in his hands. 'Serena is being looked after and she will be okay, I promise you. Here and now is for *us*. This is where we start…and go on.'

Siena looked at him, her smile growing, joy replacing the feeling of regret. 'Yes, my love.'

And then, after kissing her soundly, he drew her between his legs, wrapped his arms around her and together they watched the most beautiful city in the world emerge from the dawn light into a new day.

EPILOGUE

TWO AND A HALF years later Siena stood under the shade of a tree on the corner of the square near Andreas's parents' house. It was a fiesta day: long trestle tables were laid out, heaving with food and drink, and Andreas's extended family were milling around, children running between people's legs, causing mayhem and laughter. Flowers bloomed from every possible place.

Siena could see the bright blonde head of her sister Serena, where she sat at one of the tables. Just then Andreas's mother came past and bent to kiss her head affectionately.

When Serena had been discharged from the clinic they had brought her here and she had moved in with Andreas's parents. Receiving the unconditional maternal love that Andreas's mother lavished on everyone had done more for Serena than any amount of drugs and therapy.

They'd just bought her an apartment in Athens and she was starting a job. Every day she got stronger and better, surrounded by people who loved her.

Once Serena had been strong enough Andreas had set up a meeting between them and their brother Rocco. It had been very emotional. Rocco had regretted his harshness on meeting Siena for the first time. But now they had a half-brother, a niece and a nephew, and Siena had a best friend in Gracie, his wife. The only reason they weren't here today was because Gracie's brother was getting married in London.

Siena's eyes didn't have to search far to find the centre of her universe. Her husband and her eighteen-month-old son, Spiro, their two dark heads close together.

She could see Andreas start to look around, searching for her. She recognized that possessive look of impatience so well, and it sent thrills deep into her abdomen, where she harboured the secret of a new life unfolding.

She put her hand there for a moment, relishing the moment she would tell him later, and Andreas's head turned as he found her. Siena smiled and swallowed her emotion, and walked forward into the loving embrace of her family.

* * * * *

MODERN™

INTERNATIONAL AFFAIRS, SEDUCTION & PASSION GUARANTEED

My wish list for next month's titles...

In stores from 21st June 2013:

☐ His Most Exquisite Conquest – Emma Darcy

☐ His Brand of Passion – Kate Hewitt

☐ The Couple who Fooled the World – Maisey Yates

☐ Proof of Their Sin – Dani Collins

☐ In Petrakis's Power – Maggie Cox

In stores from 5th July 2013:

☐ One Night Heir – Lucy Monroe

☐ The Return of Her Past – Lindsay Armstrong

☐ Gilded Secrets – Maureen Child

☐ Once is Never Enough – Mira Lyn Kelly

Available at WHSmith, Tesco, Asda, Eason, Amazon and Apple

Just can't wait?

You can buy our books online a month before they hit the shops! **www.millsandboon.co.uk**

0613/01

Special Offers

Every month we put together collections and longer reads written by your favourite authors.

Here are some of next month's highlights— and don't miss our fabulous discount online!

On sale 21st June

On sale 5th July

On sale 5th July

Save 20%

on all Special Releases

Join the Mills & Boon Book Club

Want to read more **Modern**™ books?
We're offering you **2 more** absolutely **FREE!**

We'll also treat you to these fabulous extras:

- 🌹 Exclusive offers and much more!

- 🌹 FREE home delivery

- 🌹 FREE books and gifts with our special rewards scheme

Get your free books now!

**visit www.millsandboon.co.uk/bookclub
or call Customer Relations on 020 8288 2888**